The UNDERDOGS of UPSON DOWNS

The UNDERDOGS of UPSON DOWNS

CRAIG SILVEY

ALFRED A. KNOPF
NEW YORK

THIS IS A BORZOI BOOK PUBLISHED BY ALFRED A. KNOPF

All rights reserved. Published in the United States by Alfred A. Knopf, an imprint of Random House Children's Books, a division of Penguin Random House LLC, New York. Originally published in Australia by Allen & Unwin as *Runt* in 2022.

Knopf, Borzoi Books, and the colophon are registered trademarks of Penguin Random House LLC.

Visit us on the Web! rhcbooks.com

Educators and librarians, for a variety of teaching tools, visit us at RHTeachersLibrarians.com

Library of Congress Cataloging-in-Publication Data is available upon request.
ISBN 978-0-593-70363-2 (trade) — ISBN 978-0-593-70364-9 (lib. bdg.) —
ISBN 978-0-593-70365-6 (ebook)

The text of this book is set in 11.5-point Warnock Pro Light.
Interior design by Cathy Bobak

Printed in the United States of America
10 9 8 7 6 5 4 3 2 1

First American Edition

For Clare

CONTENTS

MEET ANNIE

Annie Shearer lives in the town of Upson Downs.

She is eleven years old and short for her age. She has brown hair and brown eyes.

She lives on a sheep farm with her parents, Bryan and Susie; her brother, Max; and her grandma Dolly.

People in Upson Downs think Annie is a bit different.

They think it's weird that she wears an old leather tool belt wherever she goes, even though Annie finds it useful having so many pockets to store items that can be used to fix things.

They think it's odd that they have never seen her laugh, even though she is often quite happy.

They think it's strange that they've never seen her cry, even though she is sometimes quite sad.

They worry she must be lonely, because she spends so much time by herself. But Annie cares deeply about people and quite enjoys her own company—and besides, she has a very best friend.

He is a dog.

And his name is Runt.

Annie knows she is a bit different, but she doesn't think she is weird or odd or strange. The truth is, everybody is unique. No two people are the same. Even identical twins can have different interests. And it makes the world a more interesting place.

Annie enjoys reading about exotic creatures with hidden talents.

For example, in the darkest depths of the ocean, there's a fish with a glowing flashlight poking out of its head. It's called an anglerfish.

In the forests of Australia, there's a bird that can mimic perfectly any sound that it hears. It's called a lyrebird.

In Africa, there's a frog that lives in a bubble of its own snot. It's called an African bullfrog.

And in Upson Downs, there is Runt.

Runt can't mimic any sounds, he doesn't have a light sprouting from his head, and he doesn't live in a bubble of snot, but his hidden talents *are* extraordinary.

Right now, Annie is at school.

It's a very hot Tuesday afternoon, and Ms. Formsby is

teaching the class about storms. She points to a chart displaying the water cycle.

". . . and so the vapor rises way up into the sky, where it collects and condenses into these dark clouds. And when it gets too heavy to hold on any longer, it falls back down. Which is commonly referred to as what?"

Ms. Formsby fans herself with a sheet of paper and looks at her students expectantly.

Only one hand goes up. It is Annie's.

Ken Bash, in the back corner, is asleep.

"Ken, mind answering this one?"

Ken startles awake, sits up straight, and looks around as though he's surprised to be there.

"Oh. Uh." He squints and guesses, "Three hundred and seventy-five?"

The class giggles as Ms. Formsby sighs.

"No, Ken. Math was this morning, mate. The answer is *rain*. Rain is what falls from the sky. Thank you."

Ken isn't finished.

"But three hundred and seventy-five *is* the number of days since it's rained in Upson Downs. I heard my dad say it this morning."

"Is that really true?" asks Ms. Formsby.

"Yes!" the whole class says together.

"It's awful!" says Claudia Velour, who thinks it's important to be beautiful. "I'm only allowed to wash my hair once a *month*!"

"What do you mean, *wash your hair*?" asks Fiona Grudge, who couldn't care less about being beautiful.

"My mum reckons if the drought goes on much longer, we might have to sell our farm," says Dustin Brayshaw.

"Mine said that too!"

"Mine too!"

"We just sold our place," says Ben Nguyen quietly. "We're moving to the city to live with my aunty and uncle. I don't really want to go."

Everyone feels bad for Ben, including Annie, who is in the back row, tightening a loose screw on the chair in front of her.

Fixing things is Annie's hidden talent. If something is wrong, she wants to make it right. But some problems are so tricky that it's not clear how to solve them, or they're so large that the solution doesn't fit in her tool belt.

Like the drought, for example.

Or the fact that her family might lose their home too.

A car horn interrupts the class. Everyone goes quiet. The horn honks again.

"Annie! *Annie!*"

Outside, Bryan Shearer has parked his truck on the grass beside the classroom. He is a big man, with square shoulders and a round beard.

Ms. Formsby pokes her head out of the window.

"Mr. Shearer, there are less disruptive ways to collect your daughter. I recommend the car park and the main entrance, *after* the final bell."

"It's an emergency!"

"Again? This is the third time this month!"

"Can't be helped, I'm afraid."

He honks the horn again.

In the classroom, Annie has returned the screwdriver to her tool belt and packed her schoolbag. She moves swiftly toward the door.

"Sorry, Ms. Formsby," she says. "I've already done my homework. It's on your desk."

Annie runs down the hall and through the main doors, and rushes to get into the truck.

Because there's a problem, and only she can fix it.

With Runt's help, of course.

UPSON DOWNS

Bryan drives through the main street of Upson Downs. They pass empty storefronts with window banners that say **For Sale** or **For Lease**. They pass Patel's Petals, the florist. Raelene's Relics, the antique store. They pass the bank, the butcher, and the newsagent. They pass the Golden Fleece, the only pub left in town. They pass the abandoned town hall and the deserted railway station. They pass the Big Ram, a giant statue fallen into disrepair. It has a broken horn and a damaged eye. A sign beneath it says **Thank Ewe for Visiting!**

But nobody visits anymore.

For more than a hundred years, Upson Downs was busy and thriving. Home to thousands of people and thousands more sheep, Upson Downs was famous for producing the finest wool in the world. The luxurious fleece was praised by Parisian designers and prized by tailors on London's Savile Row.

The vast plains and valleys were kept green by the deep river and meandering creeks that ran through it. It was a beautiful, vibrant place, full of wildlife and wildflowers. There were restaurants and festivals and dance halls and sporting clubs. There were stockyards and bake sales and charity events. People poured in from across the country, and Upson Downs welcomed them all.

Then everything was ruined by one man.

Bryan's rickety truck rattles along a single-lane road. Around them are brown paddocks with tufts of dry grass.

"Sorry to come and grab you early again," Bryan says.

"It's okay."

"Hope I didn't interrupt anything too interesting."

"We were learning about storms."

"Oh yeah? Could do with a few of those. You know, your grandpa Wally studied them too at one point. I remember him talking about a harebrained scheme to make his own rain clouds."

Annie turns to look at him, interested.

"Really?"

"Yeah. It was all about attracting lightning. Something about electrical currents positively charging water droplets to make them heavier. I couldn't make any sense of it. He was a deep thinker, as you know. Had a lot of wild ideas."

"Did he write it down?"

"Not sure. I wouldn't pay it much attention, though, mate," says Bryan.

It's too late; Annie is intrigued.

Bryan pulls up outside the Shearers' old timber farmhouse, bringing a cloud of dust behind him.

And there, sitting in the shade beside his timber dog-house, is Runt.

Runt is three years old and short for his age. He has brown fur and brown eyes. Annie doesn't know what breed he is. Maybe kelpie. Maybe heeler. Maybe shepherd. Maybe terrier. Maybe all of them. Maybe none of them. Annie doesn't really care. He's just Runt, and that's all that matters.

Bryan winds the window down and whistles.

"Come on, Runt! Get in!"

The dog doesn't move.

"Come on, mate! In you get!"

Runt doesn't budge.

Bryan turns to Annie. He smiles and winks.

"Always worth a try," he says.

Annie's mother, Susie, and her grandma Dolly both appear outside. Dolly coughs and waves away the last of the dust with a greasy rag. She wears a pair of blue denim overalls and a flannel shirt with the sleeves rolled up. She has short gray hair and brown leather boots.

"The dog won't listen to you, Bryan, you absolute melon! Go and get Annie!"

"I'm here, Grandma!"

Dolly stoops and squints into the truck.

"Oh! So you are."

"They haven't got out again, have they?" Susie asks.

"Afraid so."

Bryan climbs out of the truck, leaving the door open, and shoos Susie and Dolly away.

"Quick! Back into the house!"

Susie, Dolly, and Bryan all retreat and hide. Carefully, Bryan peeks around the corner of the house.

Once the two of them are alone, Runt looks at Annie, who looks back at Runt. Annie makes the faintest upward nod of her head, and Runt bursts forward, leaps into the truck, and sits happily on Annie's lap.

Bryan smiles and shakes his head.

Then he hurries to the truck, because time is running out.

THE COLLECTOR

Across the road from the Shearers' farm are hundreds of acres of lush green pasture surrounded by white wooden fences. It's a sprawling oasis, where dozens of thoroughbred horses prance about with glistening coats.

Past the iron gates of the entrance, a long driveway snakes all the way up a steep hill to an enormous sandstone manor. From here, one man surveys the parched plains of Upson Downs.

His name is Earl Robert-Barren.

His home has sixty rooms, yet Earl lives alone and has never entertained a single guest.

A staff of gardeners keeps a lawn tennis court manicured to pristine perfection, yet Earl has never picked up a racquet. The only things he has ever served are papers, because Earl is a senior counsel, which means he is a very formidable lawyer.

His estate has an expansive vineyard, and every year Earl

hires the finest winemaker in the country to handpick his grapes and craft his own vintage. Yet Earl has never tasted a glass of it. He keeps every bottle stored away in a dark, cavernous cellar.

Because Earl prefers to collect things.

Not to drink, not to enjoy, not to savor or admire. Simply to possess them.

Earl owns paintings by Pablo Picasso and Johannes Vermeer and Leonardo da Vinci and Vincent van Gogh. None of them hang on his walls. They are sealed in plastic and locked in a climate-controlled storeroom.

Earl has a library filled with the rarest books, from Dickens and Darwin to Austen and Tolstoy. He has never bothered to read a single word.

Earl has a piano that belonged to Beethoven, a bottle of Napoleon's perfume, and a quill used by Shakespeare. He has sculptures, Fabergé eggs, medieval tools, moon rocks, and hundreds of other historical artifacts.

Earl derives no joy from their beauty, and he feels no awe for their significance. His pleasure comes from owning things that other people can't have, in hiding things that they desperately wish to see. It makes him feel very powerful and important.

Earl's most treasured possession is in the center of his property. It is an enormous, deep dam filled with clear, fresh water.

It's quite easy to make a dam. Even a beaver can do it, and

they don't have hands. If you have a flowing river and a big hole in the ground, all you really need to do is build a wall.

Before Earl Robert-Barren came to Upson Downs, the river gushed from high on a ridge and spread into smaller creeks that supplied the whole town with water. Each farmer took enough for their flock, and on and on the water flowed. They relied on the river, because with every passing year it rained less and less.

Then Earl arrived. Like putting a plug in a bathtub, he blocked the river and collected all the water for himself. And down across the flat plains of Upson Downs, the creek beds dried up, the grass withered and began to die, and so too did the town.

The wool from Upson Downs declined in quality and no longer attracted the interest of Parisian designers or London tailors.

People stopped visiting. The train no longer had reason to come to town, so the station closed. Restaurants and shops struggled to make ends meet, then shut their doors for good. There were no more festivals. No more dances. No more sports.

Farmers were left with no choice but to sell their land and leave. And only one man was prepared to make a paltry offer for their dry paddocks:

Earl Robert-Barren.

Because Earl is as cunning as he is cruel.

As soon as he assumed ownership of a property, Earl installed a long pipe that reached like a tentacle from his dam, pouring water back into the empty tanks and troughs, bringing life back to the parched soil, making it instantly more valuable.

But Earl isn't interested in selling for a profit. He is collecting the town of Upson Downs, piece by piece, acre by acre. He is collecting homes and hopes and histories and lives, and he will not stop until he has them all.

THE MAGIC FINGER

Sheep have an unfortunate reputation for being quite stupid.

People believe they're dim-witted, aimless animals that are easily confused. But this is a bit unfair.

For example, sheep have very long memories. They never forget a good patch of grass, and they certainly never forget where to find a decent drink of water.

Think of your favorite food, prepared by the world's most talented chef, laid out on a banquet table that spreads out for miles. This is what Earl's pasture looks like to Bryan Shearer's sheep. It's irresistible. Which is why, despite Bryan's efforts to repair his rickety old fence, they persist in pushing their way through it, crossing the road, and squeezing onto Earl's estate.

The grass really *is* much greener on the other side. Earl's estate is paradise. They bleat and bounce about, trotting and kicking up their hooves. They stuff themselves with tufts of juicy grass, then wash it all down with a refreshing drink from Earl's dam.

And today, while Annie was at school learning about cloud formation, a storm was brewing on the outskirts of Upson Downs, because the sheep had broken out again. And Earl, peering through a brass spyglass that once belonged to the pirate Blackbeard, had spotted them.

He snatched up his telephone and poked the buttons urgently, like he was trying to wake a hibernating bear. And he yelled at Bryan Shearer for so long that he didn't realize Bryan had already hung up and left to fetch Annie.

Bryan's truck hurtles up the long driveway and stops outside the manor.

Earl stands impatiently on the stone steps. Despite the heat, he wears a double-breasted navy jacket with silver buttons and a purple silk cravat. He holds a gold pocket watch previously used by Winston Churchill.

Earl has skinny arms and skinny legs and a skinny neck beneath a skinny face. But he possesses a perfectly round protruding stomach, as though he's smuggling a wombat under his shirt.

He has a sharp nose and beady eyes, and he always looks mildly annoyed. Except right now, because Earl looks *extremely* annoyed.

In the truck, Bryan whispers to Annie and Runt.

"Stay here for now. I'll get him inside; then you two go for it."

"Okay," Annie whispers back.

Bryan gets out. He spreads his hands and smiles.

"Earl! You're looking well."

"Shearer, your merinos have yet again committed criminal trespass and are presently engaged in aquatic larceny."

"I hear you loud and clear, Earl. If we could just—"

"This is the third instance this month," Earl goes on. "You have precisely ten minutes to herd your sheep from my property, after which they will be seized under provision of the Ovine Charter."

"The Ovine Charter. Absolutely."

Bryan tries to lead Earl inside.

"What *are* you doing?" Earl complains. "Unhand me."

"I thought we might head indoors and discuss the, uh, Ovine Charter."

"You presumed to invite yourself into my house? You Shearers are incorrigible."

"I'm not sure what that means, Earl, but thank you. How about we duck around the corner here, then?"

Earl resists.

"No! I won't be shuffled about like a chess piece. I want your sheep off my property!"

"Well, here's the issue, Earl. It's just that—"

Annie interrupts, leaning out of the car. "Runt won't move if someone other than me is here, Mr. Robert-Barren."

Earl, unaccustomed to being addressed by a child, is confused.

"I've never heard of such a thing! That's absurd!"

"It's not really," says Annie. "For example, there's a type of turtle that lives in Queensland that breathes out of its bottom."

Earl stares at her, stunned. After a moment, he throws his hands into the air.

"Very well, Shearer. You may briefly enter the house, once you remove those filthy boots."

Earl swings open the large timber doors. Bryan hops up the steps, trying to shuck his dusty boots at the same time. He turns and gives Annie a thumbs-up.

When the doors are closed behind them, Annie ignites.

"Come on!"

Runt leaps out of the truck and follows Annie. He stays close to her heels as they run together.

Using her finger like a magic wand, Annie points and wags and sweeps and waves.

"Up!" she says, and Runt bounds easily over an Athenian sculpture.

"Down!" she says, and Runt doubles back, crawling under a garden bench.

"Roll!" she says, and Runt rolls over a bed of pink petunias.

"Go, go, go!" she says, and Runt dashes away from her across the lawn.

"Back, back, back," she says, and Runt returns so fast that his legs are a brown blur.

"Weave, weave, weave!" she says as they approach the vineyard, and Runt quickly zigzags between Earl's grapevines.

Runt is nimble and acrobatic and swift. Annie is like a conductor with a baton, playing him like an orchestra. It's a remarkable sight to behold, or it would be if anyone else was there to see it. But this is their own private performance, just for the two of them. It's a beautiful ballet playing to an empty theater.

"Up, up, up!" she says, and Runt hops up onto a post and delicately walks across the top of the wooden fence, keeping his balance, following Annie's magic finger.

"Down! Go, go, go! Round, round, round!" Annie says, and Runt jumps into a paddock and runs a dizzying circle around a white stallion. The horse spins and trots on the spot, pinned in place.

"Back, back, back!" And Runt returns to her, his tongue dangling out of his mouth. Annie gives him a scratch behind the ears.

"Okay, Runt. Let's go get the sheep," she says.

They find them drinking calmly at the dam. Together, the sheep lift their heads to see Runt and Annie approaching.

Their holiday is over.

They turn and charge down the steep bank of the dirt wall that traps the town's water. Then they scatter across a vast grassy paddock.

Annie points her magic finger, and Runt sprints after them.

"Get around! Go long! Back up, back up! That's it!"

Runt gallops along the fringes, blocking the path of wayward sheep and directing them toward the herd. Annie whistles and waves and shouts as she jogs behind, guiding Runt like a traffic controller.

"Hold up! Back, back, back! Get around! That's it!"

Before long, the sheep are tightly packed together, like a single creature with hundreds of legs. Annie drives them from behind, while Runt darts along the sides, keeping them locked in step.

The sheep settle down as though they've been hypnotized. Sedate and obedient, they stroll down the valley, following the path the river used to take.

Eventually, they cluster around a gate at the far corner of the property. Annie stands on her tiptoes to unhook the latch, and the sheep politely step through. Runt stalks behind, ready for a chase, daring them to split from the pack and run off. But the sheep know the drill. They march in double file, like an orderly regiment of soldiers, down a dry riverbed through the bush, back to the Shearers' farm.

Squinting through his spyglass in the office of his manor, Earl watches the last of the herd leave his estate. He checks his pocket watch.

"Just under a minute to spare," he says.

Bryan nods and smiles.

"They're a good team."

Earl takes a seat behind a big oak desk. A shelf nearby features the sculpted busts of Earl's ancestors, each wearing his own white, curly-haired barrister's wig. Six generations of Robert-Barrens, stern and humorless and cold.

One entire wall is filled with fat leather-bound books about law. Contract law, family law, international law, privacy law, water law, agricultural law, tax law, criminal law, even laws *about* law.

But Bryan's attention is drawn to an easel holding a map of Upson Downs. It shows the boundary lines of every farm in the district. Earl has marked in green every property he now owns.

Bryan's stomach drops with dread when he sees his own farm on the map, surrounded by blocks of green.

Earl snaps his fingers to get Bryan's attention.

"Mr. Shearer, any further recurrences will not be handled so charitably. The next time your sheep wander onto my land, I will be issuing a writ of ownership. Not that I particularly want them. They are a sorry-looking herd, I must say. Skinny as greyhounds. Your father would be ashamed of their condition. He had a sterling reputation for raising quality fleece; it's a shame to see it sullied. Still, the whole town seems to be in decline these days. It's a pity."

Bryan flashes with anger.

"You're right, Earl. A lot of us *are* in decline. Might have something to do with the fact that you stole our water."

"*Stole?* What is on *my* property is *mine* to keep—including your sheep, should they trespass again. My actions are perfectly aboveboard. I have always acted in strict accordance with the law. You're welcome to pursue legal action should you suspect otherwise."

"As you well know, Earl, my father tried that for years, but you delayed and adjourned and countersued and used every dirty trick until we ran out of money."

Earl leans back in his chair.

"If your financial position is dire, Mr. Shearer, I'd be willing to make a fair offer on your property."

"Nothing about you is fair, Earl. And I'd rather wear one of those ridiculous wigs than let you take my home. I'll show myself out."

Bryan doffs his hat to the row of Robert-Barren busts.

"Gentlemen."

And with that, Bryan walks out of Earl's manor.

TO THE MAX

One of Annie's favorite animals is the honey badger.

As the name suggests, their favorite food is honey and they are, indeed, badgers.

This makes them sound quite quaint and serene, but honey badgers are notable for their hidden talent: they are the bravest animal on the planet. They are so pugnacious and courageous that they seek out danger with very little concern for their own safety. A honey badger will run toward lions, sniff porcupines, stare down hippopotamuses, and chase crocodiles, despite being a fraction of their size.

Annie has a particular affection for honey badgers because they remind her of Max, her brother.

Max is thirteen years old. Like the honey badger, he has a sweet tooth. And above all else, Max Shearer is utterly fearless.

His dream is to be a famous daredevil. He films and edits his own videos for his YouTube channel, where you can see him perform such exploits as rolling down a hill inside an old tractor tire, picking up a venomous snake, exploring an abandoned building rumored to be haunted, holding his breath while submerged in a murky water trough, and riding a cranky ram like a rodeo cowboy.

Sadly, his efforts haven't yet launched him to global notoriety. So with each new video, his stunts have become more elaborate and dangerous.

And while Annie and Runt guide the sheep home and Bryan mends the boundary fence, Max is preparing to film his latest feat.

He wears a bright orange helmet from the 1980s, a pair of aviator sunglasses that cover half his face, and a dark green tracksuit with white stripes. He poses with a silver BMX bicycle and speaks enthusiastically to a camera propped on a post.

"G'day, viewers. It's Max Shearer here from *To the Max*, bringing you another wild stunt from Down Under. Today I'm taking it up a few notches. This one's called Rings of Fire. I'm gonna light up the tires of my bike, pop a wheelie, race it up this ramp here, do a wicked flip over this fence, and stick the landing. It's probably gonna be my most viral video ever. So, yeah. Um, thanks for spreading the word. Got my twenty-fifth subscriber during the week, so pretty happy with that.

Remember to chuck us a like and a comment. So, yeah. Let's get on with it!"

Max gives a thumbs-up to his audience and rolls his bike to the starting line. He kneels, strikes a match, and holds it to each tire in turn. They erupt into two flaming circles with black smoke pouring off them. Without hesitation, Max mounts the bike.

At that same moment, propelled by an instinct for her son's stupidity, or the smell of smoldering rubber, or both, Susie Shearer steps out of the house. She scans the surroundings suspiciously and sees that her son's pants have just caught fire.

"Max!"

She sprints toward him, ripping a wet towel off the clothesline as she passes. Meanwhile, Max quickly kicks off his flaming trousers before they can do any lasting damage. Susie thrashes at her son and the burning bike until the fires are extinguished.

Annie, Runt, and the sheep drift into a nearby paddock. They all stop and stare. Then Bryan arrives, a hoop of wire slung over his shoulder. He stops and stares too. He frowns at the scene: his son without trousers, his wife flogging a bicycle with a towel.

"Hey!" he calls out. "Are those my aviators?"

RUNT

At dusk, Runt sits patiently beside his doghouse.

Drooling, he looks up at Annie as she cracks open a purple tin of Mush Canine Cuisine. A wobbly, gelatinous brown tube of dog food slowly drops and plops, hitting Runt's food bowl with a wet smack that sounds like a squid sneezing.

It's a revolting mess, but it's Runt's favorite meal.

For Runt, Mush Canine Cuisine is more than food. It's love and loyalty. It's happiness and gratitude. It's home.

"Good boy, Runt. Eat it up—it's all for you," says Annie.

Runt devours the whole bowl in a couple of bites.

Nobody knows where Runt came from or how he got to Upson Downs. There were rumors that he was a stray from the city who hopped onto a freight train. Some suggested that he was an unwanted pet abandoned by the side of the road.

Others speculated he was born into a litter of wild dogs and lost touch with the pack.

Either way, one day a small brown dog arrived in Upson Downs with nobody to look after him.

He roamed the streets and did what he could to survive. He scavenged from bins behind the butcher and the baker. He nibbled at vegetable gardens and sniffed out backyard fruit trees. He stole eggs from chicken coops. He crept into the supermarket and nabbed food from the shelves. On one occasion, he wandered into the Golden Fleece and took a chicken schnitzel right off the plate.

The small brown dog was sneaky and cheeky and infamous. "That little *runt*" they called him. He was a source of irritation and consternation and exasperation. People were forever shooing him away or trying to catch him, nobody more so than Constable Duncan Bayleaf, who doubled as the local ranger.

Constable Bayleaf was obsessed. Every day he patrolled the roads in search of his elusive nemesis. Whenever he received a complaint or report of a sighting, he stopped whatever he was doing, hopped in his police wagon, started the siren, and hurtled away.

Constable Bayleaf fancied himself an outstanding athlete. There was no cover drive he couldn't chase to the boundary, no midfielder he couldn't run down and tackle, no race he hadn't won. In his career as an officer of the law, he had successfully apprehended every single criminal who had ever fled a scene.

Except one.

The dog they called Runt.

Runt was as slippery as an eel and cunning as a fox. He could dart like a rabbit, bounce like a gazelle, and climb like a monkey. He was spry and agile and clever. Constable Bayleaf would sprint after him, wielding a long pole with a rope snare at the end, but Runt would dodge and weave and feint. He would leap over cars, crawl under fences, and scale walls with ease.

People in the street would often join the chase, trying to snatch him and dive on him and trap him, but Runt slipped past them all, vanishing into the shadows like a panther in the jungle, leaving behind a parade of panting pedestrians and one thwarted constable.

As you might imagine, Runt developed a fear of people. He always kept a cautious distance. Most nights, he slept beneath the statue of the Big Ram. He shivered through the winter, and he ached with hunger.

He was all alone.

And then he met Annie Shearer.

Annie was all alone too.

Every day at school, she ate her lunch in the shade of a

peppermint tree on the far side of the oval while everyone else played. One afternoon, Annie noticed the small brown dog watching her eat from outside the school boundary. Annie waved, and the dog ducked down so that he was partly hidden in the long grass.

Annie stood and approached. Runt backed away, tense and fearful. So Annie stopped and placed half of her peanut butter sandwich on the ground and walked away from it.

Runt watched her carefully.

The bell rang and everyone ran back to their classrooms. Annie was the last to return. Before she turned the corner, she looked back. In the distance, she saw the small brown dog warily approach the sandwich, snatch it, and flee.

The next day, Runt was there again. He watched her, inquisitive and hopeful but still careful. Annie left half her sandwich again, and Runt ate it after the bell.

And the next day, Runt was waiting again. Before she ate her own lunch, she put half of it down for the small brown dog. This time, Runt didn't wait for the bell. He slowly and carefully approached, like a cat stalking its prey, watching Annie. He sniffed at the sandwich, then gulped it down and ran away.

Every day after, Annie placed the sandwich closer and closer to where she sat. Gradually, Runt became more comfortable, until one day he ate the sandwich right beside her, under the shade of the peppermint tree. When he was finished, he gave Annie an exploratory sniff, then scarpered.

The following day at lunch, Runt came up to Annie in the shade, but there was no sandwich on the ground, only Annie's empty lunchbox. Runt was confused and disappointed.

Then Annie revealed a surprise.

From her schoolbag she took out a purple tin. At ninety-nine cents each, Mush Canine Cuisine was the cheapest dog food she could buy. The photo on the label looked promising: an appetizing bowl of rich, succulent chunks of meat. So when Annie opened the tin and turned it over, she was surprised by the sad, pale tube of goop that slithered into her empty lunchbox.

Runt glanced up at Annie, unsure what to do. She worried that he wouldn't like it.

"I'm sorry—it's all I could afford," she said. "I bought it for you. I thought you might be tired of sandwiches. I hope it tastes okay. Eat up—it's all for you."

The moment she gave him permission, Runt ate hungrily. He licked the lunchbox clean. It was the most delicious meal he had ever tasted.

When he finished, he looked up at Annie and wagged his tail. It was as though he understood the depth of her kindness.

He sat with her for the whole lunch break. Then, when the bell rang, the strangest thing happened. As Annie started walking back to class, Runt followed her, right at her heels.

When she stopped, he stopped.

When she started again, he did too.

Runt followed her all the way back to the classroom.

Mr. Ranatunga, who was her teacher that year, stopped her at the door.

"Annie, you can't bring your dog into the classroom with you."

"I didn't. He just followed me. And he's not mine. I don't know who he belongs to."

Annie looked down at Runt.

Runt looked up at Annie.

And at that moment, she knew they belonged to each other.

"Either way, you need to take him outside," said Mr. Ranatunga.

Runt followed Annie to the front steps of the school.

She stopped. And he stopped beside her.

Then, for the first time, Annie used her magic finger. She held it up, and Runt sat down. There was an invisible energy that seemed to connect them. It was as though a kind of electricity moved from the tip of Annie's finger to the end of Runt's snout.

Annie lifted her finger, and Runt stepped back and stood on his haunches, perfectly balanced, like a puppet on a string.

"Wow," said Annie. "You're a clever dog."

She drew circles in the air, like a lasso, and Runt spun around as if chasing his tail. She changed direction, and so did Runt. She drew circles upright, and Runt rolled over on the grass.

Runt panted and wagged his tail.

She pointed her finger at the ground, and Runt lay down.

Annie didn't want to leave Runt, but she had to return to class.

"You're not allowed inside, but if you wait here, I'll see you after school. Deal?"

Annie held out her hand. Without hesitation, Runt filled it with his paw. They shook on it.

Deal.

Runt sat patiently until school ended and Annie returned. He stood and wagged his tail. Then he followed Annie to the car park, where her grandma Dolly was waiting.

"Who's this?" Dolly asked.

Before Annie could answer, she was interrupted by the sound of a police siren. Constable Duncan Bayleaf skidded to a stop and burst from the car clutching his snare pole. He ran into the school grounds, looking around frantically.

"Where is he?" he yelled out. "I just got a call that the runt was on school property!"

He turned and spotted Runt, who was sitting between Annie's legs.

"There!" cried Constable Bayleaf.

He marched toward Annie, a wild look in his eyes.

"Stand back!" he yelled, holding the snare like a pole-vaulter. Runt cowered and backed up. Annie didn't move.

"What are you doing?" she asked.

"Step aside, young lady. That's a wild animal."

"He's not wild," said Annie. "He's been trained. He's really amazing. Look, I'll show you."

Drawn by the commotion, dozens of students and parents crowded around. They watched with interest as Annie stepped away from Runt and held up her magic finger.

But the dog didn't move.

Annie lifted her finger. Nothing. She waved it, swished it, wagged it, zigged it, zagged it. Runt didn't respond.

"Enough!" said Constable Bayleaf.

With a quick jab, he swiftly hooked Runt around the neck.

Runt barked and struggled.

"Stop!" Annie cried out. "What are you doing?"

"I'm taking him into custody. I've been pursuing this canine for more than a year."

"Why?"

"He's a criminal element."

"He's a dog," said Dolly, getting out of the car.

"He's a bag of fleas and a public nuisance. He's responsible for hundreds of counts of theft," replied Constable Bayleaf, dragging Runt away.

Annie followed, distressed.

"Where are you taking him?"

"I'll hold him in the cells overnight; then he'll be off to the district pound in the morning."

Annie looked over to Dolly. "That's not right," she said.

"It's what happens to stray dogs, love."

"But he's my friend," Annie said.

Dolly knew how important that was. Annie had never had a friend before.

"Constable!" Dolly called out.

Bayleaf halted.

Everyone stared at Dolly. She had a commanding presence.

The animal that Annie was most reminded of by her grandmother was a lioness. They were both athletic and playful and enjoyed company. They both had thick skin and were never intimidated. They took their time and never rushed. They were protective of and devoted to their family. And they had very sharp teeth when they needed them.

Dolly Shearer walked over to Constable Bayleaf, snatched the pole from his hand, unhooked Runt, and snapped the pole over her knee.

"Your stick broke," she said, handing it back to him.

Constable Bayleaf knew better than to argue with Dolly Shearer.

And from that moment on, Runt had a home.

HUMBLE PIE

"So—what's in it tonight?"

At the dinner table, Susie serves up slices of a flat beige pie. The filling looks like a muddy pond of frogs that have vomited themselves inside out.

"Chicken giblets. Canned asparagus. Kidney beans and brussels sprouts. Got them all on special."

"Smells delicious," says Bryan, bringing his nose close to his plate. He is, of course, lying.

Susie prides herself on finding bargains at the supermarket. She scours the aisles, rescuing the food that nobody wants; then she combines it all into what she calls Humble Pie.

Most nights, the Shearers eat Humble Pie. The ingredients are always a mystery, yet the outcome is always the same: it's awful.

People often say that Susie Shearer has questionable taste.

Her personal style is as unique as it is unusual, and it's very similar to the way she cooks. Her wardrobe consists entirely of secondhand clothing. She hunts the racks of thrift shops and flea markets, rescuing the clothes that nobody wants; then she combines them into outfits.

Tonight, for example, she's wearing a long pink pleated skirt from the 1940s with a shiny turquoise blouse and a mustard-colored cardigan. She wears big wooden earrings shaped like crescent moons and a necklace made of dazzling red plastic beads the size of grapes.

Annie loves her mother's bright and vibrant clothes. They make her think of the most colorful birds in the world. They're called birds of paradise, and they live deep in the rain forests of New Guinea. Each species has its own flamboyant fashion. The birds shimmer and glisten and glow, with feathers that sprout like ribbons and plumes that burst like fireworks. In the middle of nowhere, they look the way they want to look, they are vivid and beautiful, and they are happy being themselves.

And just like Susie Shearer, they have no idea how to cook.

Max tastes his slice of Humble Pie and winces.

"It's really good," he says. He is, of course, lying too.

"It's lovely, dear. Your best one yet," says Dolly, telling the biggest whopper of all.

"You're all welcome," says Susie. "Annie, how about you?"

Annie takes a bite, chews slowly, and swallows with effort, like a snake that has to dislocate its jaw to get its meal down.

"It's a bit . . . horrible," she says.

Bryan, Max, and Dolly cover their smiles with their hands, but Susie takes no offense.

"That's okay, sweetheart. You just eat as much as you can."

The Shearers eat in silence. Annie can sense that everyone is distracted. Her whole family seems lost in their own worries and concerns, and it makes Annie worried and concerned for them.

Her instinct, like always, is to try to fix everything.

After dinner, Annie sits on her bed. Runt lies beside her, dozing.

Annie's textbook is open to a page describing the formation of storms, but Annie is studying Max's YouTube page on her laptop. He has already uploaded his latest video: "Crazy Stunt Goes Up in Flames."

It has only had two views.

Annie starts a new account and invents a user called ILoveCoolStunts. She subscribes to Max's page and leaves a comment: *Sick channel, mate!*

Annie continues to create fans, until she is interrupted by a strange series of mechanical taps and whirs coming from outside her room. Annie closes the laptop and follows the noise.

She tiptoes down the hallway, with Runt creeping beside her.

Annie peers around a door.

She sees Bryan and Susie sitting at the dinner table, which is covered with bills and logbooks and spreadsheets and documents. At the head of the table, Susie tallies up figures on an old adding machine, which spits out paper receipts that pile up around her in curls.

She tears off a long strip and hands it to Bryan. He reads through it, then puts it down. They sit quietly for a moment.

"Even if we tighten our belts another notch, I don't know how we are going to make it through the summer," says Susie.

"The overdraft on the overdraft is killing us," says Bryan.

Annie doesn't know what an overdraft is, but it sounds ominous.

"I know you don't want to, but we might have to sell the farm. If Robert-Barren offers a fair price . . ."

Bryan shakes his head.

"No. It would break Dolly's heart. All the work Wally put into this place, I can't let that come to nothing."

Bryan holds his head in his hands, and Susie rubs his shoulder.

"We just need some rain," says Bryan.

Annie retreats to her room and returns to her bed. Runt climbs up and lies down with a sigh. His snout rests on her open textbook, right beside a diagram of the water cycle.

Annie suddenly snaps her fingers. She has remembered what her dad said earlier about Grandpa Wally's invention.

"Of course," she says to Runt.

Annie takes a small flashlight from her tool belt.

Low on the wall of her room is a hinged flap of wood that leads directly into Runt's doghouse so he can come and go as he pleases.

And so can she.

They both crawl through the flap into Runt's doghouse, and out into the night.

THE DEEP THINKER

Annie might be considered a bit different, but her grandfather was believed to be genuinely mad.

Wally Shearer spent a lot of time thinking and tinkering at his workbench in the corner of the shearing shed. He wrote down all his theories and discoveries in old leather-bound journals.

He admired people who asked the Big Questions. He liked to read about philosophers and inventors and explorers. And just like Galileo and Copernicus and Isaac Newton and Nikola Tesla and Charles Darwin, Wally Shearer wasn't afraid to be mocked or cast out for introducing new ideas.

Wally lived by his own rules, one of which seemed to be a desire to relinquish his clothes. In the warmer months, he wore nothing but his hat and his leather tool belt. He roamed around the property mending fences and pipes and gates and wires and motors—because just like Annie, Wally liked to fix things.

Famously eccentric, Wally Shearer baffled and befuddled farmers across the district. But one thing they all agreed on was that his wool was the finest in the world, and everyone wanted to know his secret.

Some thought it was the quality of his grass. Others said that he must feed his sheep a special blend of vitamins and minerals. Others speculated that he sprayed them with a mysterious ointment that made their fleece grow thick and rich.

But it wasn't any of those things.

Wally's secret was happiness.

Once, on a trip to the city, Wally noticed that the men who appeared worried or hurried or miserable or stressed were all balding. He concluded that the opposite must also be true. The happier and calmer his sheep were, the thicker and richer their wool would be. So he made sure they were never hungry or frightened or alone.

Wally experimented too. That's how he learned that sheep love music.

Every day, Wally put an old windup gramophone on a fence post. The herd would gather and listen to Mozart and Beethoven and Vivaldi, transfixed by the sound.

Wally loved his sheep, and they loved him back. He never needed the company or the help of a sheepdog, because his flock followed him wherever he went.

Life was idyllic and tranquil and calm.

Then Earl Robert-Barren moved to Upson Downs and stole the water from the river, and everything changed.

Wally Shearer was faced with a problem he couldn't fix. He became worried and hurried and miserable and stressed, and he even started to lose his hair. He spent less time with his sheep, and *they* became worried and hurried and miserable and stressed. And their wool was never the same again.

Wally passed away when Annie was too young to remember. But she likes hearing stories about him, just as she likes to wear his old tool belt. She spends a lot of time at his workbench in the shearing shed. She can feel him nearby, like a comforting ghost, pleasantly haunting her.

And that's where Annie is headed now. She makes her way through the shearing shed, still ripe with the smell of old sweat and sheep manure, past the scales and the wool table and the clippers hanging on the wall. She passes Wally's dusty old gramophone. There are cobwebs in its horn.

She reaches his workbench and begins thumbing through his journals by flashlight. She flicks through years of Wally's wild notions and bright ideas.

Then she stops.

Because she has found it.

She stares at dozens of sketches. It's a strange yet simple invention. A little box with circular attachments that is placed on top of a high tower, like the star on a Christmas tree. There are corresponding phrases that Annie doesn't understand, like *Frictional Magnetization* and *Hydroelectric Conductor* and *Gyroscopic Voltage Vector* and *Magnus Force.*

There are pages of equations and explanations and instructions detailing precisely how to construct it.

But what excites Annie the most is its name:

The Rainmaker.

KIND LIES

"It's never going to work."

Max looks doubtfully at the odd contraption.

Annie has been up all night piecing materials together and constructing. She took the wheels from Max's charred BMX bike and attached empty cans of Mush Canine Cuisine along the rims. Between the two spinning wheels is an old tin toolbox filled with coils of copper wire and lined with fridge magnets.

"It's called a Rainmaker," says Annie. "Grandpa Wally invented it."

Max remains unconvinced. "You do know he was a complete fruit loop, right? He was crazy as a frog in a sock."

"He wasn't crazy," says Annie. "He was just trying to fix things."

They stand at the base of the windmill next to the farmhouse, looking up.

"So you want me to climb all the way to the top and strap it on?" Max asks.

"Yes."

"And that will make it rain?"

"Yes."

"How does it work?"

"I don't really know."

Max looks up and squints.

"I mean . . . it *is* pretty high."

Persuaded by the possibility of falling to his certain death, Max agrees to help.

"I'll do it," he says. "But I want you to film me. I'll make it part of the training montage for my next stunt. I've got something massive planned for the Woolarama Show tomorrow."

So, with Annie holding his camera, Max clambers up the frame of the windmill carrying the Rainmaker and a length of fencing wire.

Suddenly:

"Max! Maaaaaaaaaax!"

Susie bursts out of the farmhouse looking very annoyed. She holds an open schoolbag, which has been stuffed full of fabric and rope.

"Have you seen your brother?" Susie asks.

Annie turns and hides the camera behind her back. Before she can answer, Susie continues.

"When I find him, I'm going to throttle him. He's cut up my good vintage tablecloth!"

She thrusts the schoolbag out and shakes it.

"Do you know what this is? It's a homemade parachute. Can you believe it? That boy is going to give me a heart attack. *Max! Maaaax!*"

Susie marches toward the shearing shed.

Once she is gone, Max climbs down.

"Thanks—I owe you one," he says. "I've got to get that parachute back. It's a key part of my stunt tomorrow."

"She sounded pretty angry."

"Yeah, I know," he says. "Do you think it will work?"

"Your parachute?"

"No. That thing."

He points up at the Rainmaker, now secured to the top of the windmill.

"I hope so," says Annie.

After dinner, Annie stands under the windmill and looks up. The Rainmaker is silhouetted against a galaxy of bright stars. It's a clear, calm, still night. Not a cloud in the sky.

The Rainmaker doesn't spin. It doesn't rattle. It doesn't hum. It doesn't buzz. It doesn't do much of anything, really. It certainly doesn't make any rain.

Annie sighs, disappointed. She worries that she may have

followed the instructions incorrectly. But not for a moment does she doubt Wally Shearer or his invention.

Annie looks to her right and notices the lights are on inside her father's greenhouse. She walks quietly toward it.

Bryan's greenhouse is made entirely out of old windows and doorframes. The panes of glass have been frosted over, so nobody can see inside clearly. There are only strange shapes and blurry shadows.

It's especially mysterious because nobody is allowed in except Bryan, and he always locks the door behind him. He spends hours in there, mostly at night. And he never makes a sound.

Just as Annie leans forward to peek through a crack, the lights go off. The door opens, and Bryan steps outside.

He flinches and yelps when he notices Annie.

"Saints alive, Annie! I've almost soiled myself. Why are you lurking about?"

"I was trying to see what you do in there."

Bryan blushes in the dark.

"Well, that's . . . I mean . . . nothing really. Nothing important."

"Can I ask you something?"

"Okay," says Bryan warily.

"What's an overdraft? Are they bad?"

Bryan sighs. He rubs Annie's shoulder.

"It's nothing you need to worry about, mate. Come on inside. Your mum's making pies for the show tomorrow. And believe me, she needs all the help she can get."

"Because they taste so bad?"

Bryan laughs quietly.

"Well, yes. But I don't have the heart to tell her that."

"But isn't that a lie?"

"Sort of. It's more of a . . . *kind* lie."

"What do you mean?" Annie asks. "Aren't all lies the same?"

Bryan scratches his head.

"It's complicated. Sometimes it's okay to tell a lie if your intentions are good."

"Oh, I think I get it. Sort of like how Grandma Dolly always says you've got a beautiful singing voice."

Bryan laughs again. "Yes. A bit like that."

"Can I ask you something else?"

"Sure."

"Do you think she's lonely?"

"Who?"

"Grandma Dolly."

Bryan thinks about it.

In her younger years, Dolly Shearer was involved in almost every event in Upson Downs. Dance nights, choir performances, theater productions, charity drives. Above all else, Dolly loved sports. She lived to compete. In summer she was the wicketkeeper for the cricket team, and in football season

41

she was a ferocious ruck-rover. If anyone on the field took issue with the fact that Dolly was a woman, she soon set them straight with a crunching tackle or a six over midwicket. Dolly also set records at the golf club, the tennis club, the bowls club, the badminton club, the bridge club, and the darts club.

When Wally passed away, it left a hole in all their lives, especially Dolly's. And at the same time, the town was shrinking. One by one, all the clubs folded; then the town hall closed its doors.

And Dolly had nowhere to go.

Recently, she has been looking for love again. She regularly attends senior singles nights throughout the district, and she has posted advertisements in the personals section of the newspaper. She has even tried online dating on an app called Widowr, but the right person still hasn't come her way. It doesn't stop her searching, though. Dolly Shearer has never been one to give up easily.

Now that he considers it, Bryan realizes that Annie might be right. Dolly *is* lonely. It makes his eyes well up with tears. He blinks them away and sniffs.

"No, mate. I'm sure she's just fine," he says.

Annie senses that he isn't telling the whole truth, but it's hard to tell if it's a Kind Lie or an Ordinary Lie.

"Can I ask you another question?"

Bryan shakes his head.

"That's enough for tonight. Come on, Detective Shearer. Big day tomorrow."

SHOW BUSINESS

The Woolarama Show attracts thousands of people every year. It is held on a huge flat paddock surrounded by gum trees, and it's a very busy affair.

There are carnival rides, bouncy castles, bumper cars, a dunk tank, slippery slides, a haunted house, a hall of mirrors, and games of chance. There's a rodeo arena, farm equipment exhibitions, talent shows, equestrian events, log-chopping contests, and, of course, sheepshearing competitions.

And there is a *lot* of food.

Near the middle of the fairground, there's a long row of stalls that fill the summer air with the most sumptuous and succulent scents. People refer to it affectionately as the Gastric Bypass.

It's a smorgasbord of delicious delights. For the sweet tooths, there are vendors selling fairy floss, toffee apples, ice cream, slushies, chocolate bars, chocolate cakes, and chocolate milkshakes. There are fresh doughnuts, butterscotch-caramel popcorn, waffles with syrup, toasted marshmallows, lamingtons, pavlovas, honeycomb, and an assortment of lollies.

Farther down the lane, there is fried chicken, hot chips, buttered corn, roast crackling pork, barbecue ribs, dozens of different curries, dozens of different pasta dishes, dozens of different noodles, and dozens of different tacos. There are steaming pans of paella. There are hot dogs. There are burgers.

And right down the end, under a saggy tent, are the Shearers, selling their Humble Pies.

Susie wears a bright red gingham dress and a vivid blue apron. Annie is out front with Runt, offering free samples from a tray. She is largely ignored, until she finally arouses the interest of a large man who is already holding a banana split in one hand and a roasted turkey leg in the other. Even so, he can't resist the opportunity.

With some careful maneuvering, he pinches a morsel of pie and puts it into his mouth. Immediately he stiffens as though he's been bitten on the backside. He swallows heavily. Then he coughs so hard, he drops his turkey leg.

"What on earth is in that?" he asks, gasping for air.

"Canned mackerel, parsnip, cabbage, and prune," says Susie proudly.

"It tastes like sh—"

"Shearers' Pies!" Max interrupts from behind the trestle

table. "Shearers' Humble Pies! Rave reviews! Best pies in town, they reckon! Get them while you can!"

The man retrieves his turkey leg from the ground, blows off the grass and grit, and takes a bite. He shakes his head and moves on.

"Strange man," says Susie. "Anyway, do either of you know where your father is?"

"He said he forgot something and was heading back home to get it," Annie answers.

"And what about Dolly? She seems to have disappeared too."

Annie and Max look at each other and shrug.

Bryan is inside the Agricultural Pavilion.

It's a vast shed. One half is home to prize pigs and ducks and chickens and rabbits. The other half is filled with rows and rows of plants. There are giant pumpkins, heirloom carrots, and ripe tomatoes. There are intricate tulips, delicate daffodils, and frightening Venus flytraps. In every section, one plant has been awarded a blue ribbon.

Bryan hides behind a maidenhair fern. He watches nervously as three stern-looking judges turn their attention toward a row of rosebushes. They speak in low voices and mark their grades on clipboards.

They reach the very last rosebush. Bryan holds his breath.

The judges stop and look at each other in wonder. It is an extraordinary specimen.

The flowers are big and lush and perfectly formed, but that isn't what makes the rose remarkable.

Each petal on each flower is a different color. From velvety black to rich crimson to pearly white to ocean blue to royal purple to canary yellow to flamingo pink and every hue and tint in between. Each flower forms a glorious bouquet, and from it wafts a perfume that is sweet and fruity and zesty and luxurious.

The judges each fondle a flower, making sure the rose is not a hoax or a fake, because they have never seen or smelled anything quite like it.

They scribble quickly on their clipboards.

And Bryan crosses his fingers.

The first Woolarama Show was held over a hundred and fifty years ago, and some traditions have stood the test of time.

Like the kissing booths, which started in the 1930s as a way to raise money for a regional children's hospital. It remains a popular attraction and is still a fundraiser for charities. Anyone is welcome to occupy a booth and volunteer to be smooched.

Today, one of those volunteers is Dolly Shearer.

If she's honest, Dolly is less interested in charity than in luring a potential love interest, but so far she's been as popular as Susie's Humble Pies.

It certainly doesn't help that in the booth beside her is Derek Tingle, an oat farmer from Dumbleyung who is widely considered the handsomest man from here to the sea. Rumors abound that Derek was once a cover model for romance novels. He has big white teeth, his shirt is open to his navel, and the queue to kiss him snakes all the way back to the petting zoo. At this rate, Derek could raise enough money to cure every sick child in Australia.

A couple of teenage boys wander past. They point and laugh when they see Dolly.

"Don't lose your dentures, Grandma!"

"Still got my original chompers, mate. I can't promise the same for you if you give any more of that lip. You'll be on the ground lookin' up."

Stunned and slightly afraid, the teenagers move on.

Dolly sighs and quietly loses hope.

Susie sighs and quietly loses hope.

She beckons Annie over and speaks to both her children.

"All right, you two, we're not exactly run off our feet. Why don't you take a break and I'll hold the fort."

"Are you sure?" Annie asks.

Before Susie can answer, Max takes his chance and slips out the back of the tent.

Susie smiles.

"I'm sure. You and Runt go enjoy yourselves."

Annie and Runt stroll along the grassy alleyways. It's busy and loud, and people brush past them from all sides. It makes them both uncomfortable, so Annie leads Runt away from the crowds, toward the farthest side of the fairground. She ducks behind a row of tents, then turns down a narrow lane.

It's much quieter here. They drift past a palm reader and a vegetable juice stand and a stall selling creepy puppets. Then Annie hears a cheer and a round of applause. She turns a corner, and down the end of a path she sees a crowd of spectators.

Ordinarily, Annie would walk the other way, but she feels a strong magnetic pull. Curious, she approaches.

The audience stands five or six deep around a roped-off area the size of a basketball court. Annie strains on her tiptoes but still can't see.

She takes a deep breath and squeezes through to the front. Runt follows close behind.

Before them is a strange sight.

Annie's first thought is that it's an odd-looking playground. There's a seesaw, and a balance beam, and two low tunnels made from shiny fabric. There are sticks poking out of the ground in a tight row, a suspended hoop, and other unusual obstacles.

Annie notices Runt becoming restless beside her. He shifts on his paws, as though the ground is too hot. He pants and wags his tail.

Then everything changes.

On the far side, an energetic border collie appears from inside a white marquee, alongside a middle-aged woman wearing a visor. Behind them is another woman. Her name is Viv Richards, and she walks out carrying a loudspeaker. It squeals as she makes an announcement.

"Folks, next up we've got Angela Dunn and Ziggy, all the way from Garranyabba."

The crowd claps. Ziggy the border collie sits obediently behind a white line while Angela stands a few meters away. Viv holds a stopwatch and begins a countdown.

"Three . . . two . . . one . . . *go!*"

At a wave from Angela, Ziggy springs forward. Angela runs ahead and guides him through the elevated hoop, then around a sharp turn and over a high hurdle, under a low bar, up the seesaw, where he teeters at the midpoint until the plank tips and hits the ground, before sprinting through a tunnel, then weaving between the thin poles.

Annie and Runt watch, completely still, utterly spellbound.

Ziggy glides over a long jump, doubles back through the other tunnel, leaps up and over a balance beam, then dashes across the finishing line.

Viv clicks the stopwatch.

The audience cheers and applauds in appreciation.

"46.27 seconds!" Viv exclaims. "Well done, Ziggy and Angela. That puts you into sixth place overall. Great effort! Give them another hand, folks."

It is then that Annie notices the big banner hanging from the roof of the white marquee. It says:

Woolarama District
Open Canine Agility Course Competition
First Prize: $500

Annie's eyes go wide.

Five hundred dollars.

It sounds like a lot of money to Annie. She wonders if it's enough to pay for the overdraft on the overdraft. Maybe not, but it would certainly help. She looks down at Runt, who is looking back up at her.

Suddenly, there is a loud bang.

Just a few meters away, at the edge of the course, a confetti cannon has been fired into the air. A tall man wearing a purple velvet tracksuit strides through the cascade of colored paper and onto the course. A nervous gray whippet follows, wearing a matching velvet coat.

Behind them, a short man, who appears to be a very obedient assistant, presses Play on a boom box. A dramatic orchestral score fills the air.

The man in velvet takes a deep bow. Then he removes his track jacket and tosses it behind him. His assistant scampers out and retrieves it.

The crowd is confused. They look at each other with raised eyebrows as the man performs a number of deep stretches.

Viv walks over and stops the music. Then she talks through the loudspeaker.

"Righto. I think that's probably enough of that. Ladies and gentlemen, our next contender is no stranger to agility course competitions. He comes from a long line of successful handlers, and he's a *fifteen*-time national runner-up. Please welcome Fergus Fink and his dog, Chariot!"

After an awkward silence, a couple of people clap softly.

The assistant, whose name is Simpkins, leads the whippet to the starting line and removes her velvet coat.

Fergus Fink takes his position in the center of the obstacle course. He stands like a matador, head high, proud and dramatic.

Silence.

Annie concentrates. She wants to remember *exactly* how to run the course, because she has had an idea.

Viv counts down.

"Three . . . two . . . one . . . *go!*"

Fergus sweeps his arms and Chariot dashes onto the course. The dog is swift and clinical, negotiating the obstacles without paying much attention at all to Fergus, who prances about like an improvisational dancer, twirling, spinning, leaping. He lunges forward and snaps back. He reaches out as far as he can and wiggles his fingers. At one point, he drops onto one knee and swings his arm in a wide circle, like a rock-star guitarist.

Meanwhile, Chariot is a blur of professionalism, zipping through the tunnel, dipping neatly between the pickets, jumping, darting, turning, then sprinting across the line.

The crowd applauds Chariot for her outstanding run.

Fergus Fink responds as though it's a stadium ovation just for him.

"I know, yes. I know. You're welcome. You're all *very* welcome. You must be so impressed."

As he bows and blows kisses, Viv Richards steps forward with the loudspeaker.

"And Chariot takes the lead with a time of 41.08 seconds! That will be hard to beat, folks, especially since that's the last of our scheduled participants. Remember, though, this is an *open* competition, so anyone can enter. It runs for another thirty minutes, and walk-ins are welcome to have a go!"

The crowd starts to disperse. Annie summons her courage and approaches the white marquee.

Nearby, Fergus Fink is furious. He rants at Simpkins and Chariot, his face the color of a sunburned pig.

"41.08? Outrageous! That's three seconds slower than my personal best! If you think I'm taking this horrendous form to the National Titles, you can think again! I know we're in some filthy, uncultured backwater, but I have a reputation for perfection, and I will accept nothing but the best. Simpkins, you're not training this mutt hard enough. I should put *both* of you in the crate tonight after you run drills."

Ashamed, Simpkins and Chariot both look down at the ground.

At that moment, Viv appears, and Fergus Fink immediately changes his tone. He smiles.

"Ah, Viv. There you are. Now I'm off to my trailer for a massage and a fizzy water. I'll return to collect my trophy and prize money at the presentation. Come along, Chariot. Heel, Simpkins."

Fergus Fink turns and pushes past Annie, barely noticing her.

Viv watches them depart. She rolls her eyes.

"Excuse me," Annie says. "We'd like to enter, please."

"Sure!" Viv says cheerfully. "Just write your names on the board over there. The competition fee is twenty dollars."

"Oh," says Annie, deflated. "Twenty dollars?"

"That's right. First prize is five hundred. And it's a hundred each for second and third. The top three qualify for the National Titles in the city."

Annie thinks hard. She only has $1.65 in her tool belt.

Then, of course, there is the other problem: Runt.

"Would it be okay if you asked everybody to leave before we had our go?"

"What do you mean?" Viv asks.

"Just . . . so that nobody could watch us."

"Well, it's a popular event, I'm afraid, love."

Annie understands. She nods and thanks Viv.

Two big problems that need two big fixes. Annie walks and thinks and thinks and walks.

Then she looks up. In the distance, she sees Max moving quickly, on a mission. He is wearing his orange helmet, his homemade backpack parachute, and Bryan's aviator sunglasses. Annie snaps her fingers. She knows what she needs to do. She catches up to him, with Runt running alongside.

"Max, wait! Do you think you could create a diversion?"

"What do you mean?"

"Do you think you could draw everyone's attention to one place?"

Max looks momentarily confused. He points at his backpack with his thumbs. "Why do you think I smuggled this in with me?"

Then he runs off. Annie watches him weave his way through the crowd.

With that problem apparently fixed, Annie turns her attention to the next.

She dreads it. Solving this one is going to be incredibly difficult, and not because she doesn't know what to do. It's because in order to do what she thinks is right, she must do something she knows is wrong.

*　*　*

Bored, Susie watches people walk past and ignore her Humble Pies.

Annie enters through the back of the tent.

"It's okay, Annie. There's no need to come back. I don't know why, but nobody seems to want my pies."

Annie steps forward. On the table is an open biscuit tin with money for customers who need change. She sees a five-, a ten-, and a twenty-dollar note. She breathes quickly. Her face feels hot. There's a lump in her throat that makes it hard to swallow, and her heart thumps fast.

Exasperated, Susie gives up.

"That's it," she says. "I'm going to read my book."

Susie bends and rummages around in her handbag.

As she does so, Annie reaches out and takes the twenty-dollar note, stuffing it into her tool belt just as Susie stands up straight.

"Go on," says Susie, shooing Annie away with her paperback. "Get out there and enjoy yourself."

Annie leaves the tent. She feels guilty and awful as she quickly makes her way back to the agility course.

"If we lose, I promise I'll pay it all back," she says to Runt.

Runt replies with a bark and wags his tail.

TAKING THE PLUNGE

You may be unfamiliar with the spectacle that is competitive log chopping, which is just as well, because it's one of the most irresponsible and dangerous pursuits ever devised.

If you were to write an actual recipe for disaster, your key ingredients might be brute force, something very sharp, and a race against time. Combine all three, and you've got an accident waiting to happen.

And that's precisely what a Log Chop is.

There are several different events, but the aim is usually the same: to be the first person to chop a block of wood in half with an axe.

The safest is the Standing Block, which involves a stump that has been clamped vertically about waist high. The race is a flurry of strong arms and wood chips. A skilled axe wielder can hack through a block of timber the width of a dinner plate in just a few seconds.

Slightly *less* safe is the Underhand Chop, which positions the stump sideways, inches from the ground. A competitor then stands on it like a skateboard, swinging the axe hard and fast between their feet.

This is, as you might imagine, quite perilous.

There have been many injuries and mishaps over the years at the Woolarama Log Chop. The most famous of these occurred in 1963 when Jed Eggers, competing in the Underhand Chop, slipped and sliced clean through his ankle with such force that his foot tumbled all the way to the front row of the crowd. Within seconds, a curious magpie swooped down and attempted to fly off with it.

The incident made the national papers. The following day's headline was **Horrific Axe-ident at the Woolarama Leg Chop!**

Fortunately, Jed and his foot were both saved. Jed even returned the following year to compete. His foot returned too, but it was no longer attached to his body. It had been pickled and preserved in a mason jar, and it became the official trophy of the Woolarama Log Chop.

Surprisingly, the *most* dangerous and precarious event doesn't involve an axe, or anything sharp.

It is called the Hundred-Foot Pole Climb.

Just as the name suggests, it requires scaling a pole that is one hundred feet high. What the name *doesn't* suggest is that there is no safety harness, and the goal is to race the competitor beside you.

Like the timber workers of old, the climbers have only the assistance of a slack hoop of rope that they use for purchase as they scamper upward. Once at the top, the climbers slide back down, where a padded mat lies to break their fall. The first to touch the earth again is declared the winner.

It is absurdly treacherous and requires immeasurable courage, which is why it's Max Shearer's favorite feat of all.

Max was five the first time he saw the Pole Climb. Every year since, he has watched in wonder as his heroes defied death. And every year, he made the same promise: that one day *he* would climb to the top.

And today is that day.

There are two poles at the Woolarama Show. They tower over the eucalyptus trees behind them like giant goalposts.

Max stands at the base of one of them and looks up in awe. His moment has finally come. He encircles the pole and his waist with a length of rope, then ties the ends together.

Nearby, the audience for the Log Chop is starting to assemble. People mingle and chat and find their spots. Nobody notices Max as he tightens the straps of his backpack, leans back against the rope, and, without a moment of hesitation, begins climbing the pole.

It's easier than he expected. In just over a minute, he is halfway up, which is also the moment that a woman in the crowd spots him.

She stands and yells and points.

Then the people around her stand and yell and point.

Then the people around *them* stand and yell and point. The news ripples out like wildfire. All over the fairground, people stop what they're doing and rush to the Log Chop arena.

Blissfully unaware of the commotion below, Max Shearer is having the time of his life.

He climbs and climbs and climbs.

Annie and Runt weave through the tide of people walking in the opposite direction. Annie clutches the stolen twenty-dollar note in the pocket of her tool belt.

By the time they reach the agility course, the crowd has vanished.

"I don't know how you did it, but thank you, Max," Annie whispers.

She finds Viv and hands over the money.

"I'm Annie, and this is Runt. We'd like to enter the competition, please."

Viv checks her watch and puffs her cheeks.

"Made it in the nick of time. You're the last run of the day. Come on through."

Runt follows Annie under the boundary rope.

"Have you two competed before?" Viv asks.

"No, never."

"Just lots of practice, then."

"Sort of," says Annie.

"Well, it's an open tournament, so there's no heats and no finals and no second chances. It's once around the course, best time wins. Got it?"

Annie nods. But there's still one more small problem.

"Is it okay if you don't watch us?"

Viv frowns in confusion.

"I'm afraid I have to, Annie. I've got to adjudicate and time your run. Why do you ask?"

"It's just . . . Runt won't go if anyone else is watching."

"Stage fright, eh?"

"I guess."

Annie glances around. Inside the open marquee is a large whiteboard with the names and times of each competitor. She points to it.

"Maybe you could stand behind that and peek round the side?"

"You want me to hide behind the whiteboard?"

"Yes, please."

After a moment of hesitation, Viv Richards smiles and shrugs. *Why not?* she thinks. After all, it's the final run of the day—not to mention the fact that this young girl and her scruffy, uncollared dog are hardly going to break any records.

So Viv steps behind the whiteboard. She peeks around the edge with her stopwatch poised.

"I'll do the countdown!" Annie calls out.

She walks Runt to the white line and holds up her magic finger.

Runt sits. He waits obediently while Annie steps into the middle of the arena. She takes a moment to look around and confirm the order of the obstacles.

Then Annie holds her finger up to the sky and looks at Runt.

"We can do this, Runt. You're amazing. I know we can beat them."

Annie is certain. She isn't nervous. She isn't afraid.

She counts down.

"Three . . . two . . . one . . . *go! Go! Go! Go! Go!*"

Annie waves, and Runt blasts away from the starting line. Annie guides him through the hoop, turns him around, and points him over the hurdle. Runt then slips easily beneath the bar and scales the seesaw, where Annie halts him halfway to wait for the plank to land. He sprints down the slope and zips through the tunnel.

Behind the whiteboard, Viv's jaw drops. She can't believe her eyes.

"Left, right, left, right, that's it!"

Annie coaches Runt through the slalom, which he executes with ease.

"Hup! Hup!"

Runt soars over the long jump.

"Get around, get around, down here!"

He zooms through the tunnel again, even faster the second time.

"Here, Runt! Careful."

Runt expertly steps across the balance beam.

"Go, go, go, go, go!"

And he bolts for home, crossing the finishing line.

Viv clicks the stopwatch. She looks at the time.

Stunned, she slowly steps out from behind the whiteboard. Annie and Runt stand together, looking across at her expectantly, full of hope.

METEORIC FALL

"First prize!"

Bryan says it quietly to himself and whistles.

He reaches out and touches the blue ribbon attached to the winning rosebush.

"Isn't it exquisite?"

Bryan is startled by the voice behind him. He spins around. It is Gretel Patel, who owns Patel's Petals, the florist shop in Upson Downs. She wears a beautiful green sari, which is as bright as her smile. She steps forward.

"I have been waiting all afternoon to meet the magician who created this beautiful plant."

"Is that so?" Bryan gulps.

"I would pay top dollar for this masterpiece. It is precisely what our town needs, don't you think? More colors, new ideas. But sadly, look . . ."

Gretel points to the label card beside the rose. Under "Entrant" it says: *Anonymous.*

"It seems there is a mysterious genius in our midst. A true enigma."

"I dunno about that," says Bryan.

"Why do you suppose they are so secretive about their identity?"

"Maybe he's just a bit shy about it all," says Bryan, clearing his throat. "Or maybe he's got other responsibilities, you know, so he feels a bit guilty about all the time he spends on it. Or *she,* of course. Or *they.* I mean, *whoever* it is."

Gretel Patel smiles again.

"I didn't know you had an interest in the botanical arts, Mr. Shearer."

Bryan blushes and bumbles. "Who, me? Nah, not my thing. I just wandered over to see if I could buy some cheap veggies."

He swivels and looks around. That's when Bryan notices the Agricultural Pavilion is completely deserted. He frowns.

"Where *is* everyone?"

Dolly is in the kissing booth, fast asleep.

Susie is in the pie stall, reading her novel.

Annie and Runt are at the agility course.

And Max Shearer is at the top of a hundred-foot pole.

He sits on it as casually as on a kitchen stool, looking around in amazement. From up here, he can see the whole fairground, the car park, the bushland, the paddocks, and the horizon beyond.

Directly below, he can see that everyone is packed into the Log Chop arena, staring up at him. He smiles and waves.

Max is too high up and giddy to notice how tense and frantic the crowd is down there. At the foot of the pole, police and paramedics and volunteer firefighters are rushing to lay down protective mats.

"No need!" yells Max. "I've got my own parachute! I'm gonna do a base jump!"

They can't hear Max, and Max can't hear the chorus of voices urging him to climb back down.

A huge tarpaulin sheet has now been carried out and unrolled.

Dozens of people clutch the edges and pull it taut. They stare upward, ready to catch Max if he falls.

Meanwhile, one of the competitive pole climbers has embarked on a rescue mission, steadily ascending the pole to retrieve Max and bring him down safely.

All this does, of course, is spur Max into action.

He takes out the cotton tablecloth from his backpack, to which it is tied with thin ropes. His idea is to fling the parachute out like a fishing net and drop underneath it, floating gracefully to safety below. Max isn't worried in the slightest about whether his parachute will work, because he has practiced at home by tossing an egg attached to a pillowcase from the roof of the shearing shed, and most of the time it worked fine.

The climber is gaining quickly, just seconds away.

Max gets to his feet.

At ground level, people gasp.

Max takes a deep breath.

He gathers the fabric, tosses it up into the sky, and leaps.

For the briefest moment, Max feels he is suspended in time. Like a soaring eagle, or a kite on a breeze.

But this is quickly replaced by a feeling of profound regret. Not, as you might imagine, because his life is in imminent danger, but because he has just realized that he forgot to set up his camera to film the stunt.

Oh no, he thinks.

His parachute, meanwhile, does very little to slow his fall. Max plummets toward the earth like a meteor wearing a long scarf.

The crowd below winces and flinches. They cover the eyes of their children. They put their hands on their heads as they watch the boy drop from the sky.

The people gripping the tarpaulin brace themselves.

Thump!

Max Shearer smacks into the middle of the tarpaulin. It bows inward with the impact.

A hush falls over the crowd. They peek between their fingers. They stand on tiptoes. They wait with their breath held.

Slowly, Max appears. He stands unsteadily.

There's a collective exhale. Sighs of relief fill the air.

Max rattles his head. His helmet is askew. The aviators are bent out of shape, and a lens has popped out.

Then he grins.

"That was *wild!*" he says. "*Please* tell me someone filmed that!"

To his surprise, the crowd hasn't burst into applause. Instead, they seem to be looking at him in horror. Specifically, they are staring at his arm. Curious, Max glances down, and he immediately understands why. His arm has snapped at the elbow and is hanging like a Christmas stocking.

"Oh," he says. "That's not good, is it?"

THE BIG FIX

The crowd has returned to the agility course for the prize presentation. Among them are all the entrants. There are dozens of dogs of different shapes and sizes, and dozens of handlers of different shapes and sizes.

Inside the roped-off area, Annie and Runt stand beside Fergus Fink. On a table are two small plaques and one big silver cup. Fergus sighs and taps his foot. He is smugly impatient, as though everyone has gathered just to see him lift his trophy.

Viv Richards barks into her loudspeaker.

"Congratulations to all the participants this year. It was a fantastic competition, and the standard was very high. Now, without further ado, let's get to the winners! In third place we have Peri Wilson and Rufus with their run of 42.38 seconds! Well done, Peri and Rufus. Come forward."

There is polite applause as Peri, who was standing to the left of Annie and Runt, steps up to collect her small plaque and an envelope containing one hundred dollars. Rufus, a cheerful Irish setter, does not care at all about the prize and is more interested in investigating the morsel of food that just slipped from the hands of a nearby child.

Fergus Fink checks his watch, bored and annoyed by the lack of attention being lavished upon him.

"Now, second place," says Viv, "is *quite* an upset this year. It's absolutely extraordinary, really."

Fergus looks down at Annie and raises his eyebrow.

"Runner-up, eh?" he says. "And with *that* dog! My word, that *is* extraordinary. Well *done*. You must be *very* proud." He rolls his eyes sarcastically.

"Second place goes to . . ." Viv pauses, relishing the moment. "Fergus Fink and Chariot with their run of 41.08 seconds!"

The spectators murmur in surprise and disbelief.

It takes Fergus a few seconds to absorb what has happened.

He blushes bright red and stays where he is.

"I'm sorry, dear. There appears to be a shocking error. You've just read out *my* name for *second* place, not first. I'm afraid you're—"

"Absolutely right!" Viv pushes the second plaque and an envelope into Fergus Fink's chest.

She turns to the crowd.

"And I'm delighted to announce that our Woolarama District champion this year, who came out of nowhere with one of the fastest runs I've *ever* seen, is a local girl from Upson Downs, just eleven years of age. It's Annie Shearer and Runt with a time of 40.15 seconds. That's a new course record for the Woolarama Show!"

The audience claps and cheers. Viv is thrilled for Annie. She grins as she hands over the silver cup and an envelope with five hundred dollars stuffed inside. Annie thanks her politely and tucks the envelope into her tool belt. Viv kneels to offer Runt a celebratory pat, but he backs away and hides between Annie's legs.

"He doesn't really like being patted," Annie explains.

"Fair enough. Well, Annie and Runt, I think the two of you are something special. Congratulations!"

Predictably, Fergus Fink is shocked and outraged.

"40.15 seconds? *This* mutt? *That* little girl? Impossible. I don't believe it. This is a conspiracy! I demand a rerun. This can't be right. The Canine Agility Course Association will be hearing about this. Simpkins! Begin drafting a formal complaint. There are shenanigans afoot. Shenanigans!"

Simpkins takes a pen and notepad from his back pocket and scribbles briskly.

Nobody pays Fergus Fink any attention. Viv drowns him out with the loudspeaker.

"All three have qualified for the National Titles. And remember, the top two dogs in Australia earn an invitation to compete at the prestigious Krumpet's Dog Show in London, which boasts a grand prize of a quarter of a million dollars!"

Annie's eyes go wide.

A quarter of a million dollars.

That's more money than she could ever fit into her tool belt.

Annie looks down at Runt, who looks up at her.

That's it. That has to be enough to pay the overdraft and save the farm.

She's finally found it. The way to fix all their problems.

PIED AND SNEAK

Annie returns to the pie stall.

Before she enters, she hides her trophy under an empty cardboard box behind the tent.

Inside, Susie is distressed.

"Annie! Thank goodness you're back. It's all gone pear-shaped. Somebody stole twenty dollars from the till! It must have happened while I was distracted with my book."

"I'm really sorry," says Annie.

"Oh, it's not your fault, love. I should have been paying more attention. The thing is, they didn't even steal a pie! Not even the thieves want them. It's a disaster."

"I'm sure that the money will—"

Susie interrupts, lost in her rising anxiety.

"And your brother has just managed to snap his arm like a twig, so I've got to get to the first-aid tent to see how he is. I don't know where Dolly has been all day, and your father seems to have fallen off the planet. So I need you and Runt to stay with the stall, please. Thank you for being so lovely."

Flustered, Susie grabs her bag, kisses Annie on the head, and leaves.

Annie watches her go, feeling terribly guilty.

It seems that in trying to fix one big thing, she has caused all sorts of smaller problems along the way.

She can't repair Max's broken arm, but she *can* try to mend her mother's broken heart.

She looks at the biscuit tin. She looks at the trays of pies. Annie snaps her fingers. An idea has formed.

She picks up as many pies as she can carry and slips out of the tent. Then, as quickly and secretly as she can, Annie disposes of them before running back to the stall for more. She feeds pies to a pen of prizewinning pigs. She slips them into handbags and show bags and diaper bags. She drops them into the round holes of a whack-a-mole game. She floats them in the water of the lucky duck pond. She balances them on the posts of the coconut shy.

Runt helps too. He digs a shallow hole behind the dunk tank, and Annie lays half a dozen pork liver and prune pies to rest. Runt buries them by pushing dirt with his snout, and Annie tramples the ground flat.

Finally, hurrying along with the very last pie, Annie turns a corner and runs straight into someone. The impact knocks her to the ground.

She looks up.

It is Fergus Fink.

The pickled gooseberry and French meringue pie slides slowly down his velvet tracksuit and splats on the ground.

Fergus is frozen with fury. Beside him, Simpkins is quick to take out a monogrammed handkerchief from his own pocket. He shakes it out like a waiter with a napkin and begins wiping Fergus down.

Annie is breathless. Fergus narrows his eyes. His lip curls into a sneer.

"*You,*" he snarls.

"I'm very sorry," Annie says.

Fergus glares at her, then at Runt, then back at her.

"Which one of you do they call Runt?"

"I'm Annie. This is Runt."

"I know *that*. I was being clever and cruel."

"Oh."

Frustrated, Fergus Fink snatches the handkerchief away from the fussing Simpkins, getting sticky meringue all over his fingers.

"Well, *Runts.* I will see you both at the National Titles, and this time it will be run fairly and squarely. You won't best me again, mark my words."

Fergus marches away, with Simpkins and Chariot trotting behind.

Annie climbs to her feet and rushes back to the stall.

Every single pie is gone. Annie takes the five hundred dollars from the envelope in her tool belt and fills the biscuit tin.

The moment she closes the lid, Susie returns.

"Max is going to be fine. Your father has gone with him to the hospital, and they should be home later toni—"

Susie stops. She blinks hard.

"Where are all the pies?"

"I sold them," says Annie. She opens the lid of the biscuit tin and shows Susie the stack of money. "Look!"

Susie is too stunned to speak.

"Plus, I found twenty dollars under a tea towel. It must have blown out of the tin."

"You mean you sold them *all*?"

"Yep. Every single one. There was a really big rush. People said very nice things about them."

Susie's jaw drops. Then her mouth spreads into a smile. She beams, looking happy and relieved and proud.

"Wow," she says. "They really *do* like my pies!"

THE GLOW IN THE DARK

Annie lies in bed, her mind crowded with thoughts and problems and hopes and worries. They keep her awake.

She gets up, careful not to wake Runt, who is snoring blissfully beside her. Annie leans down and gives his head a soft kiss. Then she crawls outside through the doghouse and walks over to the windmill. She looks up at the Rainmaker.

It hasn't moved an inch.

It's another clear, cloudless night. The stars are a spray of sparkling glitter.

Annie sighs and puts her hands into the pockets of her tool belt.

"I don't know why it's not working, Grandpa Wally," she says softly. "I followed the instructions, but maybe I did something wrong. Maybe it takes a while to get going. I guess I'll just be patient. But I have another idea that might help save the farm."

"Who are you talkin' to?"

The voice in the dark belongs to her dad.

"Grandpa Wally," says Annie.

Bryan squeezes her shoulder.

"Come with me."

Annie follows Bryan across the yard, all the way to his greenhouse.

He unlocks the door and opens it.

To Annie's surprise, he invites her inside.

She enters. In the murky darkness, the first thing she notices is the extraordinary aroma. The air is pungent and perfumed and fresh and sweet. It's as though she's inhaling color through her nostrils.

Annie follows Bryan down a shadowy center aisle. She can feel things lightly brushing her skin. It makes her flinch and shiver.

At the other end, Bryan flicks a switch, and everything is revealed in a sudden golden glow.

Annie can't believe her eyes. She is inside a beautiful garden. A perfect oasis, so lush and green compared to the dusty brown paddocks around it. She looks around in wonderment. It's a jungle of potted plants. Some are arranged in orderly rows, some are on shelves, some are on the ground, some hang from the ceiling. There are tiny seedlings. There are strange pots with twigs sprouting from them. There are shrubs bearing exotic fruits that she has never seen before. There are orchids shaped like butterflies and violets with bursts of vivid purple and yellow. There are ugly succulents and intricate bonsai and a plant whose tiny flowers look like ladybirds.

And standing on a long bench is Bryan's rainbow rose-bush, with a blue ribbon proudly pinned to its pot.

The bench is home to strange items: long tweezers, glass droppers, jars with powders and potions, spray bottles, scissors, clippers, delicate brushes, magnifying glasses, and small envelopes.

Then Annie sees it.

On the bench, hiding behind the rose, is a silver cup. It is her agility course trophy from earlier in the day. She forgot all about it.

Her stomach drops. Annie suspects she is in a lot of trouble.

Bryan slides it in front of her.

"I think this is yours," he says.

Annie stares at it for a moment.

"I think I told some Kind Lies today," she says.

"I think you're right. It's okay—I know what you did, Annie."

"How?"

"Because I'm a brilliant detective. See, your mother mentioned earlier that she thought twenty bucks had been nicked from the till, and then at the end of the day there was an even five hundred in there: those sums happen to be the entry fee and the first prize for the agility course competition."

"Oh."

"Also, I ran into Viv Richards when I went back to pack up the stall, and I couldn't shut her up about you and Runt."

"I'm sorry."

"You don't need to apologize, mate. You don't even *want* to know what your brother got up to today. I know why you did it, Annie. And don't worry, I won't tell your mum about the money. Besides, we've all got our little secrets." Bryan points to his rainbow rose.

"What are all these plants?" Annie asks.

Bryan shrugs. "Bit of an interest of mine, you could say. Some experimental propagation, a bit of creative grafting."

"What's grafting?"

Bryan kneels beside a plant that looks like a strange sculpture made of sticks. There is a main branch, with twigs sprouting from it that are bound in place by string.

"Grafting is when you blend one plant with another, and then another, and another, and create something new. This one's in the early stages, but look here."

Bryan beckons her over to a leafy shrub with reddish fruits the size of golf balls.

"What is it?" Annie asks.

"This"—Bryan plucks one and hands it to her—"is a peachummery."

"A peachummery?"

"A peachummery."

"I've never heard of it."

"That's because this is the only one in the world. It's a peach and a plum and a cherry all in one."

"Can I taste it?"

"Of course you can."

Annie takes a bite. Her eyes go wide. It's juicy and tart and sweet and soft and ripe.

"It's delicious! And a bit weird."

"Isn't it? Come look at this."

Excitedly, Bryan picks up a small plant from the ground and places it on the bench. It has plain white flowers and looks otherwise unremarkable.

"Ready?" Bryan asks.

Annie peers at the plant, slightly confused. She's not entirely sure what she should be ready for.

"I think so," she says.

Bryan switches off the lights.

Annie blinks hard in the dark.

"I'm not sure what I'm supposed to be looking at."

"Wait for it. . . ."

As Annie watches, the petals of the plant begin to glow white, then blue, then green, then white again.

Annie gasps in wonder. It's beautiful.

"Bioluminescence," Bryan says. He leans in close to the

plant, which casts just enough light for Annie to see him smiling. "Attracts nocturnal pollinators."

He switches the light back on, and the spell is broken. The plant looks unremarkable again.

"That's *really* amazing," says Annie.

"I like it too. But this one here's my pride and joy," Bryan says, sniffing his rainbow rose fondly. "Took me twenty years to cultivate. Hundreds and hundreds of grafts, dozens of different varieties. I ordered seeds from all over the world and grew them and put them all together. You know, it's a bit like Runt, eh? He's a real mutt, no telling what breeds he might be, and he's something very special."

"That's true," says Annie.

"You know, Viv reckons you two could take the National Title. She said your time was world-class."

"I don't think it's possible."

"Well, you've just got to practice, I s'pose."

"No, I mean . . . Runt won't run with all those people watching."

"Ohhh, of course. That *is* a tricky wicket."

Bryan drums his fingers on his chin, but he is out of ideas.

"You know who would know what to do?" he says. "Grandpa Wally."

"That's true."

"He didn't happen to answer back, did he, when you were talking to him out there?"

"No."

"It's a shame. I could use his help too sometimes."

"*I* can help you," says Annie.

"You already do, love. You know, maybe we can find a trainer for Runt. Someone who specializes in strange animal behavior. Maybe they can sort your brother out while they're at it."

"Okay."

"But that's for another day. It's bedtime, champion. And don't forget your trophy."

"You're a champion too," says Annie, pointing at Bryan's blue ribbon.

Bryan raises his eyebrows, as though it has just occurred to him.

If there's one animal her dad reminds Annie of, it would be the giant panda. It's a big, friendly, hairy bear that loves plants and moves at its own pace and doesn't ever hurt anybody.

"Yeah, I s'pose I am," says Bryan with quiet pride. "By the way, where did you put all those pies?"

"Well, I . . ." Annie pauses. "Do you *really* want to know?"

Bryan laughs loudly.

"No, maybe I don't. I've had enough surprises today."

SCARECROWD

A seesaw built out of an old weatherboard plank balanced on a stepladder.

A slalom of cricket stumps and golf clubs poking out of the ground.

Tunnels fashioned from cardboard boxes that have been taped together.

Hurdles made from rusty gates.

A hoop jump that used to be a motorcycle tire.

An A-frame ramp made from bent corrugated iron, with a crusty rug thrown over it.

A balance beam constructed from fence posts.

Together, it becomes Annie Shearer's Backyard Agility Course, all laid out in a flat, dusty paddock outside the farmhouse.

Every afternoon for weeks, Annie and Runt practice on their improvised course.

The Shearers peek through the curtains, marveling at the two of them. Especially Max, who is Very Grounded.

Housebound, with his broken arm encased in a plaster cast, Max watches Runt sprint and leap with a mix of envy and awe.

He has taken to secretly filming them through his bedroom window. He is particularly impressed by Runt's warm-up tricks. Following Annie's finger, Runt runs up the side of the water tank, backflips, and lands on his feet. He rolls over dozens of times in a row, as though he's tumbling down a steep hill. He spins around and around, kicking up a dizzy tornado of dust. He balances on his back legs and steps backward. He catches tennis balls and twists in the air. He weaves between Annie's legs as she walks. He jumps onto her back and springs up and over her head. Sometimes they even play hide-and-seek. Annie closes her eyes and counts to ten while Runt sprints away to conceal himself. As hard as she looks, she can never find him. Annie has to give up and call his name, and Runt reappears like a magic trick.

Then they get to work, running their circuit over and over and over again. Runt never gets tired, and he never slows down. Each time Runt crosses the finishing line, Annie checks their time on a Casio digital wristwatch she found in the shearing shed.

When the sun has set and they are finished for the day, Annie gives Runt a scratch behind the ears and the same piece of encouragement as they walk back to the farmhouse, dirty and sweaty.

"Good job today, Runt. But I reckon we can do better tomorrow."

In the evenings, Annie sits on her bed with Runt and watches past Grand Championship performances from the Krumpet's Dog Show on her laptop.

She studies every run carefully. The dogs look sleek and refined, and the course is so proper and professional. It's a million miles away from Upson Downs and their dusty practice paddock. Still, intimidating as it is, Annie knows they can beat them.

There's just one problem.

The Krumpet's Dog Show is held in an enormous stadium packed full of spectators. In the arena there are judges and officials and referees and camera operators. It would be impossible to clear them all out.

The only way to win is for Annie to fix Runt.

One thing that gives Annie hope is that Runt has already been practicing in front of an audience of hundreds.

Every day, the sheep gather up and down the fence line to stare at them. The herd is very confused, but they're also quite relieved that he's not devoting his energy to chasing them.

Runt doesn't seem to mind the sheep watching. But as soon as Dolly steps out to collect the washing, or Bryan appears from the shearing shed, or Susie opens the back door to ask if Annie has finished her homework, Runt stops on the spot. He sits, and he will not move an inch until they are gone.

When the coast is clear, he comes to life again.

And Annie sighs and shakes her head, confounded.

Looking for answers, Annie researches phobias.

She reads about a woman who shrieked at the sight of bananas. There was a man who was too scared to look into mirrors. There were people who were frightened of butterflies, pickles, mushrooms, chins, the color red, the number eight, and, more commonly than Annie would ever have expected, clowns. *Lots* of people were terrified of clowns.

It seems that if a thing exists, *somebody* in the world is afraid of it.

Suddenly Runt doesn't seem so unusual.

Annie looks for stories about people who managed to overcome their fears. She reads about Henri Menteur, a boy from Paris who, a hundred years ago, was so frightened of bicycles that he wouldn't leave the house lest he encounter one. His parents took him all over France to specialists who gave him medicines and ointments and tonics, but nothing seemed to work.

Then he met a doctor who prescribed nothing more than a pencil. He told the boy to draw the tiniest bicycle he could, no bigger than a postage stamp. Henri did as he was asked. Then he looked at it. The bicycle was so small that, although he felt uncomfortable, he didn't fear it.

The doctor told him to draw a new bicycle every day, each one slightly bigger than the last.

All winter long, Henri sketched bicycles and pinned them on his walls. By the spring, his room was covered with them. The last bicycle he drew was the size of his bed.

And it worked.

Not only was Henri cured, he became *obsessed* with bicycles. By the end of the summer, he had a newspaper route and pedaled all over Paris delivering them. Ten years later, he competed in the Tour de France.

This gives Annie an idea.

First, she constructs a cardboard silhouette of a person and paints a friendly face on it, placing it on the edge of their practice course. After a skeptical sniff, Runt pays no attention to it.

So she adds a new one every day.

Annie's fake audience grows more elaborate. She makes scarecrow people out of stuffed stockings and burlap bags, dressing them in worn clothes and spraying them with perfume or cologne. Their heads are made from balloons that bobble in the breeze. And Annie chats with them to fool Runt into believing they are real.

Bryan finds a couple of plastic mannequins at the rubbish tip, and Susie donates a tailor's dummy that she dresses in a colorful outfit. Max offers some of his posters of rock bands, which Annie pins to the fence.

Using Grandpa Wally's old cassette player, Annie records crowd noises from sporting events and concerts, and she plays them on a loud loop while they train. It doesn't slow Runt down at all.

So Annie decides it's time for phase two of her plan.

It's time to introduce some *real* people.

One week out from the National Titles, while Runt is distracted by a bowl of Mush Canine Cuisine, Susie, Dolly, Bryan, and Max sneak into the practice paddock and stand like statues beside the cutouts and dummies and balloon-headed scarecrows.

Dolly takes her place beside a striking mannequin. She raises an eyebrow.

"Come here often?" she asks.

The mannequin doesn't respond.

"She must be shy," Dolly says to Max.

The Shearers stand still and straight and silent.

Once Runt has licked his bowl clean, he follows Annie down to the agility course.

Annie stops him at the starting line. Then she holds up her magic finger. Runt obediently sits, and Annie steps into the middle of the course. Her heart beats fast. She glances at her family, who are frozen in place and staring straight ahead like wax dolls. She feels a glimmer of hope.

Runt, meanwhile, turns his head on an angle and appears to squint in Bryan's direction. Bryan gulps and sweats. His nose itches.

Annie takes a deep breath.

She holds her finger high.

"Three . . . two . . . one . . . Let's go, Runt! *Go! Go! Go!*"

But the dog doesn't move. It's as though he hasn't heard a word.

Instead, he scratches at his ear with his back paw.

"Come on! Go, go, go, go!"

Annie waves and jumps and skips on the spot, but Runt doesn't budge.

Annie sighs.

"Sorry, love," Susie whispers out of the corner of her mouth, still holding her frozen pose.

Deflated, Annie feels her shoulders slump.

"It's okay," she says. "You can all leave."

The Shearers collectively exhale. They move off their

marks. Bryan gives Annie's arm a sympathetic squeeze as he passes.

Once the course is clear and nobody is watching, Annie lifts her magic finger. She counts down from three and sweeps her arm.

And Runt launches into action.

However, somebody *is* still watching.

On a distant hill, peering through a pair of long-range binoculars, is Fergus Fink.

Simpkins stands close by, holding the binoculars to his employer's eyes, because Fergus is cradling a white Persian cat that purrs contentedly in his arms.

Fergus, who has watched the entire afternoon unfold, now steps back and arches an eyebrow.

"*Very* interesting," he says.

PEDIGREE

"**Pedigree**" **is a funny** word for a silly idea.

Dogs have pedigrees. Racehorses have pedigrees. Sheep have pedigrees. And, according to some, people have pedigrees too.

Pedigree is the belief that if your parents were clever and wonderful, and your parents' parents were magnificent too, and your parents' parents' parents were also brilliant, then simply by being born, you must be just as clever and wonderful and magnificent and brilliant as them.

This is, of course, complete garbage.

It doesn't matter how impressive your parents are, you can still be a disappointing dud. The opposite is also true: the most woefully odious and awful people can produce delightful, talented, and kindhearted children.

It's only people who are convinced *they* have pedigree who seem to think it's important. They like to gaze back on the achievements of their family and feel very good about themselves, as though they had anything at all to do with it.

Fergus Fink, for example, is proud of his pedigree.

So much so that he expects to be treated like an elite champion at all times, because he firmly believes that he was born better than everyone else.

It is certainly true that he comes from a long line of Finks. And the Finks, it must be said, have a very famous name in the canine agility course community. They are, indisputably, very successful dog handlers and trainers.

Since the events were first established, every generation of Finks has won both the National Title and the Krumpet's Dog Show's Grand Championship.

From Ferrick Fink in the 1920s to Fignacious Fink in the 1930s to Fergaline Fink in the 1940s to Finnigan Fink in the 1950s to Farrington Fink in the 1960s to Funklin Fink in the 1970s to Furbert Fink in the 1980s to Frida Fink in the 1990s.

Then it was Fergus Fink's turn to take the leash.

But since then, no Fink has won at home or abroad.

Fergus has competed every year, and has finished second fifteen times. He is forever the runner-up, the silver medalist. And every year that he fails, the pressure to succeed weighs heavier. He feels the disapproval of the entire Fink family. It makes him bitter and resentful and desperate, yet somehow also further convinced of his own brilliance.

The way Fergus sees it, his lack of success is no fault of his own. He blames his trainer, Simpkins, and *especially* his dog, Chariot, whom he loathes.

The truth is, Fergus detests *all* dogs.

He considers them crude and revolting creatures. When they're not rolling in filth, they're barking at nothing in particular, or scratching themselves, or sniffing unspeakable smells, or licking things they shouldn't be. Fergus looks down upon dogs as stupid and blindly loyal. As far as he is concerned, they are a weak animal in search of a strong one to obey.

This is why he admires cats above all other living things.

A cat is a creature of stature and poise. Fergus enjoys their high opinion of themselves and their refusal to follow instruction. A cat isn't interested in behaving in a way that will earn your affection, because a cat's expectation is that you will stop what you're doing and attend to it the moment it desires attention. A cat doesn't jump through hoops or walk up planks or run through tunnels unless it wants to, and even then it will be done at its own leisure. Cats won't follow anybody unless there's something in it for them. Cats won't be tamed. Cats tame you.

Furthermore, a cat will hide patiently, for hours if necessary, just for the chance to leap out and remind you that, if it so chooses, it can and will murder you, and the only reason you're alive is because it's allowing you to be.

Fergus Fink has twelve cats. And no friends.

His closest human companion is Simpkins, who cleans, cooks, and serves his every whim. And this year, Fergus has insisted that Simpkins train Chariot twice every day.

This is no chore for Simpkins. He loves dogs, and he adores Chariot in particular. He never pushes her too hard, and he is quick to praise and pat her. He bakes his own bone-shaped treats to reward her with, and he massages her after their practice sessions.

Fergus doesn't bother attending practice until the eve of a competition, when he half-heartedly waves Chariot through the circuit, checks the time, and then claims credit for Simpkins's hard work and Chariot's performance.

"I'm a champion," he says. "It's in my blood."

And he believes it, because Fergus Fink believes in pedigree. And to him, that means he has a destiny to fulfill. Because pedigree can be more than who you are. It can also determine what you do.

Consider any royal family. Kings and queens have princes and princesses who become kings and queens who have princes and princesses. And on and on it goes.

Throughout history, it has been common for children to take over a family business. To be a baker or a blacksmith. A miner or a seamstress. A professional dog handler . . . or a sheep farmer.

That is why Annie Shearer has been thinking a lot about

pedigree recently. And family. And inheritance. And living up to a legacy.

Not because of Runt and who his parents might have been.

Annie has been thinking about her dad.

She thinks about him in his greenhouse with the door locked. His big thick fingers holding those tiny tweezers and that delicate little brush, peering through a magnifying glass at petals and leaves. She thinks about how proud he looked beside his plants and his flowers. Inside his greenhouse oasis, he wasn't stressed about the overdraft or worried about the drought. He seemed much happier in there than out in the paddocks with the sheep, and she wonders if that's why he keeps it all a secret.

NO GOOD, NO GOOD, NO GOOD

"Uno!"

Two days out from the National Titles, the Shearers are playing cards around the dining room table. Max, his arm still in a cast, has won again.

Susie collects their discarded hands and shuffles the deck.

"What's going on, Annie? You usually trounce us at Uno."

Annie shrugs.

"I still haven't found a way to fix Runt, and I'm running out of time. I don't know what to do."

A thoughtful silence falls over the table. Then Dolly snaps her fingers.

"Remember Meredith Croydon? She ran the bookshop before they had to sell up a few years back. Pretty little woman. Dull as a bowl of oats. You might recall her husband,

Harold, drove that Mercedes everywhere. He thought he was the bee's pajamas. Wore leather gloves just to drive it down the road to buy milk. I mean, *please,* spare me. Deirdre Spinnaker bumped his taillight with a shopping trolley and, oh, heavens above, you've never seen somebody so hopping mad. I thought he was going to burst."

Bryan reaches across the table and grabs Dolly's hand affectionately.

"Mum, I love you dearly, but if you don't get to the point of this story, *I'm* going to burst."

"Righto. Yes. What was it? Oh. That's right. I remember Meredith had a spitz called Fritz that was a glutton for her dirty socks."

"Did he swallow them?" Bryan asks. "Or did he spitz them back out?"

The whole table rolls their eyes at Bryan.

Dolly continues. "She took Fritz to a hypnotist in Parchment Creek, and it worked like a charm. Too well, truth be told. The dog's now terrified of feet."

"Actually," says Susie, "that reminds me. I read about a holistic animal behaviorist in the paper a while back."

Max perks up, suddenly excited.

"*Ballistic* animal behavior?"

"*Holistic. Hole.* Not *ballistic.*"

"Oh." Max is disappointed. "What's *holistic* mean?"

"It means . . . I have no idea what it means. I think it's a spiritual thing. She runs weekend retreats for retired service dogs and troubled pets."

Max makes a face, unconvinced. "Sounds a bit stupid," he says.

Susie raises her eyebrows and her voice. "I'm not sure you're in a position to make any judgments about stupidity, are you? Have *you* got any bright ideas, other than lighting yourself on fire or jumping off a building? Should we tie Runt to a rocket? Or all put our heads in a shark's mouth?"

Max, who is, technically, still in A Lot of Trouble, knows from the tone of his mother's voice that it would be unwise for him to contribute anything further to the conversation. He shrugs and hides his arm under the table.

"Well," says Bryan, changing the subject, "I've done some reading too."

"Really?" Annie and Susie and Dolly ask together.

"Yes, *really*," says Bryan, a little offended. "Bernadette Box. Heard of her?"

The Shearers shake their heads.

"Not even you, Annie?"

"No, I've never heard of her."

"Interesting," says Bryan, sounding quite pleased with himself. "Bernadette Box won five consecutive agility course National Titles back in the nineties. And then she never competed again. Fell off the radar. Completely disappeared. But here's the thing: I looked her up, and she only lives a couple of hours away, up in the blufflands. Maybe she knows a thing or two."

Everyone looks at Annie.

"Can we try to visit them all tomorrow?" she says.

Bryan nods once.

"Worth a shot, I reckon."

Tick. Tock. Tick. Tock.

Dr. Werner Gruyère is a very skinny and very bald man with vivid blue eyes that stare through round wire-rimmed spectacles. He wears a yellow short-sleeved shirt and a caramel-brown tie.

Annie and Runt sit uncomfortably in front of his oak desk. The only sound comes from a grandfather clock in the corner of the room.

Tick. Tock. Tick. Tock.

On the wall behind Dr. Gruyère are a painting of a Swiss Alp and a photograph of him standing on the crest of a mountain with a Saint Bernard. They both look very serious.

Annie has been in his office for ten minutes and she has yet to see him blink. It makes her eyes itchy.

"So," says Dr. Gruyère, "you are wanting to free this dog from his terrors."

"I don't know about that. I just want to help him be able to do things while other people are around."

Dr. Gruyère stares at her. "Performance anxiety. A curious pathology. We must go deep."

"Deep?"

"Deep into his unconscious mind. This is where the truth resides. In our waking hours, we are all liars."

"I'm not sure if that's—" Annie attempts to disagree.

"Every cause has a root. Every reaction has an action. Every end has a beginning. We must unlearn what has been learned. We must undo what has been done. We must journey to the source."

"Okay," says Annie, although she hasn't understood a word.

"To do this, we must go *deep*."

Finally, he blinks. Slowly. Like a reptile.

Then Dr. Gruyère abruptly stands.

"Please," he says, pointing to a leather couch.

Warily, Annie moves across the office to sit on it. Runt follows her.

Dr. Gruyère takes an umbrella from a stand beside the door. He opens it, revealing a large black-and-white swirl pattern. Looming in front of Runt, he twirls the handle of the umbrella, creating the illusion of an endless tunnel. His voice is soft and low.

"You are running, running, running, through fields of wheat and barley, but you are getting very tired, yes? Very heavy in the legs, so you are slowing, slowing, slowing, and then walking in a little circle, around and around, finding a place to rest, because you are very tired, very heavy. When I snap my fingers, you will lie down and sleep."

The umbrella stops spinning. Dr. Gruyère snaps his fingers.

Runt doesn't move.

Dr. Gruyère snaps his fingers again. And again.

"You will lie down and sleep."

Snap. Snap. Snap. Snap.

Runt looks up at Annie. Annie looks down at Runt.

Then they hear a loud thump.

They turn to see Dr. Gruyère on his back, sprawled on the floor.

Snoring.

Outside, Bryan waits in the truck, listening to the cricket on the radio.

The passenger door opens. Annie and Runt climb inside.

"*Already?* That was quick. How'd it go?"

"No good."

"No good?"

"No good."

Pearl Fernleaf wears purple robes, and her earrings are small feathers. She smells very herby. She also believes that she can communicate with dogs using their language.

Annie and Runt sit on thin mats in Pearl's meditation tent,

which is lit by candles. Pearl sits opposite them, legs crossed, eyes closed. Completely silent.

Then her nose twitches. She begins sniffing the air. A moment later, her mouth opens and her tongue appears. Pearl pants loudly.

Annie is as confused as Runt.

They both flinch as Pearl suddenly springs onto her hands and knees. Her hips wiggle, wagging an invisible tail. She rolls a ball toward Annie with her chin. She barks; then she waits.

Tentatively, Annie tosses the ball. Pearl scurries after it, yapping.

Runt watches her as though she is a brand-new species.

Pearl gives up trying to retrieve the big ball with her small mouth and runs up to Runt, sniffing him up and down. She barks again and rolls onto her back, legs in the air, tongue out. She twists over and crouches. She looks very alert, listening hard, as though someone in the distance has called her name. Then she tilts her head back and howls.

Runt looks at Annie. Annie looks at Runt.

Finally the howling stops. Pearl closes her eyes. She nods once.

She opens her eyes and looks surprised, as though she's been asleep for hours.

"Are you . . . okay?" Annie asks.

"Annie, this dog is *very* unusual."

"The *dog* is unusual?"

"Very. He's resisting me. I can't commune with his ancient energies."

"Oh, okay. Actually, I don't really know what that means."

"We all carry the stories of our past lives, Annie. But Runt is shrouded in secrecy. There's so much tension blocking his voice."

"I'm not sure that helps me to understand."

Pearl Fernleaf opens a velvet drawstring bag and takes out a thin crystal rod, the thickness of a pencil.

"So, first, I must clear his pathways."

"His what?"

"His pathways. So if you could just lift his tail for me . . ."

Runt, as though sensing the destination of the crystal rod, narrows his eyes and issues a deep warning growl.

Bryan is reclining, boot dangling out the open window of the truck, half asleep.

"Go! Go! Go!"

He awakens, blinking hard.

"Start the car!"

He rattles his head and sits up straight. Squinting, he sees Annie and Runt running toward the car. There's a strip of purple fabric hanging from Runt's mouth.

He starts the car just as Annie and Runt jump inside.

"Go! *Quick!*"

Bryan quickly accelerates away.

"No good?"

"No good."

After traveling for more than an hour across flat, parched pastures, they reach the thick forests of the blufflands and begin climbing its steep hillsides. Annie stares up at the tall trees through the window, occasionally checking the large map on her lap.

Eventually, she guides Bryan onto a narrow dirt road, and they follow winding, bumpy tracks into the heart of the bush, bouncing about on their seats as shrubs and branches scrape the sides of the truck.

Finally, they arrive.

Bryan stops a few meters away from a gate covered with intimidating signs.

Keep Out! Private Property! No Trespassing! No Visitors!

Beyond it is a yard overgrown with weeds and covered with junk and scrap material, and beyond that is a small, slumping, ramshackle cottage in dire need of repair. The golden afternoon sun drops down below the trees, casting a cool, dark shadow.

"Last chance," Annie says to herself.

Bryan peers at the cottage, worried. "Are you sure this is it?"

Annie double-checks the route she traced onto the map. "I think so."

"I reckon I'd better go with you this time," Bryan says.

The three get out and slowly approach the gate. All is quiet, except for the insects and the birds.

The moment Bryan touches the latch of the gate, a voice yells out.

"Clear off! No thank you! Not interested! Leave me alone! Goodbye!"

It's not immediately clear who is shouting, but Annie briefly glimpses a woman at the window. Then the curtain falls and she is gone from view.

Bryan sighs.

"No good, I guess. Come on, mate. I don't think she wants to be disturbed any more than she is already."

They trudge back to the truck. Bryan rubs Annie's shoulder as he reverses out.

"Sorry, love. Three strikes, eh?"

But Annie is deep in thought.

"Wait," she says.

She has had an idea.

Bryan brakes.

"What's the matter?"

Annie hops out of the truck.

"Let me try something."

Bryan opens his door.

"No," says Annie. "You stay there."

"Are you sure? Be careful!"

The gravel crunches underfoot as Annie and Runt approach the gate again. Annie looks hard at the yard, taking careful note of everything in it.

Cautiously, she unlatches the gate and they step onto the property.

The curtain behind the window draws back slightly.

Then Annie takes her chance.

She lifts her magic finger and points Runt into action. She weaves him between a slalom of tall weeds. She guides him underneath a broken plastic chair and over a stack of milk crates, then turns him sharply through a tunnel of blackberry vines growing over the rickety fence.

"Hup! Hup!"

Runt leaps and clears a rusted bathtub.

"Hup! Wait! Down, down, down."

Runt climbs a pyramid of firewood, teeters at the top, and runs back down. He is swift and sure. Annie makes a hoop out of her arms, holding it out to the side, and Runt sails through it.

Then he suddenly skids to a stop.

And he sits, completely still.

Because standing outside the cottage, watching, is Bernadette Box. She is short and tough and wild. She wears a ripped denim shirt, and her baggy trousers are patched. Her arms are folded.

"You must be Annie Shearer."

Annie is taken aback. "Um . . . yes."

"And this must be Runt."

"How did you know?"

Bernadette doesn't answer. She turns around, walks up the wooden steps to the porch, opens her front door, and disappears inside.

Annie watches her go, disappointed that her plan didn't work. She looks down at Runt.

"I guess she just wants to be left alone."

They begin walking back to the gate.

Then the door swings open and Bernadette reappears.

"Well, are you coming in or not?"

THE BOND

In a surprising contrast to the haunted and unwelcoming look of the cottage from the outside, Bernadette's lounge room is cozy and neat.

Annie stands beside a low fire that crackles in the fireplace as she waits for Bernadette to return from the kitchen. She looks around with great interest, admiring the gold trophies on the mantelpiece. The walls are covered with framed photos of a young, smiling Bernadette and a black Labrador. There are news articles too. Annie reads the headlines:

> **Stunning Debut!**
> **Boxie and Moxie Win Again!**
> **Unbeatable!**
> **Pawfection!**
> **Record Breakers!**

Then she sees a front-page article that says:

Shock Retirement Stuns Canine Community

Bernadette returns with a clattering tray of tea and biscuits.

"My dad told me you were a champion."

"It was a long time ago," says Bernadette. "That's all behind me now."

She sets the tray down and fondly watches Runt, who circles before finally lying on the rug in front of the fire.

"That's where Moxie used to curl up," says Bernadette wistfully. "That exact spot."

"You two must have been an amazing team," says Annie, still marveling at the display on the walls.

Bernadette wants to change the subject. "Why don't you have a seat?"

"Okay."

Annie looks around, then lowers herself onto a small wooden footstool, because Bernadette only has one chair.

"Sorry," says Bernadette. "I don't entertain very often."

Annie thanks her for the tea. Then, because there aren't any on the tray, she takes two sugar cubes from a pocket of her tool belt and drops them into her cup. Bernadette watches her curiously.

"Tell me more about the pair of you."

Annie takes a sip. Then she tells Bernadette the story of

Runt. How the people in town gave him his name. How they chased him and tried to catch him. How the two of them met, how they became best friends, and how he follows her everywhere she goes.

Once Annie starts talking, she can't stop.

She tells Bernadette about the drought and the empty river. She tells her about Earl Robert-Barren, about her farm, about the Rainmaker and Grandpa Wally. She tells her about the overdraft on the overdraft, and her plan to win the National Title so she can win the Krumpet's Dog Show in London and fix everything.

By the time her tea and her tale are finished, Bernadette is so moved that her eyes are shiny.

"That's why I need your help," says Annie. "Because you're a champion."

"*My* help? You don't need my help. Annie, there's only one true secret to becoming an agility course champion. No amount of training can produce it, and in the end it matters more than any trophy. And you two have already got it."

Annie leans forward on her little stool.

"What is it?"

"The *bond*. The magnetic connection. The love and respect you have for each other. Runt knows where you want him to go before you've even thought of it."

"Was it the same with you and Moxie?"

Bernadette looks up at a photo of Moxie on the wall. She nods, looking both proud and sad.

"Did you win the Krumpet's Dog Show too?" Annie asks.

"We never went."

"But you qualified. How come you didn't go?"

Bernadette shrugs.

"Moxie didn't like to travel. It made her very anxious. She hated to be in that dark little crate, all on her own. She would bark and whimper so much that it broke my heart. I don't doubt that we could have won over there, though. She was brilliant."

Annie nods.

"It's kind of the same thing with Runt," she says, "and I don't know what to do. You saw him before. He gets scared as soon as someone is watching, and he just shuts down. That's why I came to you, I suppose. To see if you had any advice for me. There's going to be lots of people at the National Titles, and even more in London. How did you get Moxie to overcome her fears?"

"I didn't," says Bernadette bluntly.

"You didn't?"

"No. I never asked her to. I accepted it. To me, it wasn't worth it. I wasn't going to force her, or cause her distress. I couldn't ask her to be someone she wasn't."

"Oh," says Annie. "Is that why you retired?"

Bernadette takes a deep breath and shakes her head.

"When I lost my friend, it was just too painful to go back. And I couldn't bear the thought of training another dog. It just made me miss my Moxie. We shared something special.

I'm still connected to the sport, though, in my own way. That's how I knew about you. But I'm a bit like Runt; I prefer to avoid too many people at once."

Annie looks up at Bernadette. She understands exactly what she means.

If Bernadette Box were an animal, Annie reckons, she would be a ground pangolin, which looks a bit like an ant-eater. Ground pangolins live in deep burrows all on their own, and they wear a scaly suit of armor to protect themselves. If they feel threatened, they roll themselves into a tight, hard little ball so they can't be harmed. They might look grumpy and suspicious on the outside, but ground pangolins are very gentle and quite friendly once they trust you.

"I was worried you might be mean," says Annie. "But you're nice."

There is a loud knock on the door, and they both flinch.

"Hello? Annie?" Bryan peeks through the screen door. "Hello? Everything all right?"

Annie stands. "We should probably go. Thank you for the tea."

Bernadette nods and smiles, though she seems sad to see Annie leave.

They walk down a creaking hallway. Annie and Runt step outside.

"Sorry," says Bryan. "Didn't mean to interrupt. But you'd been gone for a bit, and I was just making sure you weren't in a cauldron being turned into stew."

Bernadette raises her eyebrows.

"No offense, of course," Bryan stammers, clearing his throat. "Just with the signs and everything, you know . . ."

Annie turns.

"It was very good to meet you."

Bernadette nods.

"Likewise. And it was good to meet you too, Runt. Good luck tomorrow, Annie."

Bernadette Box watches them walk away. She smiles seeing Runt following Annie with such intimacy and loyalty. She can see that they are inseparable.

As the gate opens, Bernadette feels an urgent flurry in her chest.

"Annie!" she calls out. "Wait!"

Bernadette waves her over. Annie comes running back, her tool belt flapping against her hips.

"Did I forget something?"

"No, no."

Bernadette kneels down, looks Annie in the eyes, and speaks quite softly, so only she can hear.

"I just wanted to tell you that I don't think Runt is afraid. In fact, he looks like a very brave dog indeed. For a long time, he didn't have anyone. And then you found each other, and you showed him kindness when nobody else ever did. That's why he follows you everywhere. He chose you. And you chose him. That's why you're such a brilliant team. As far as Runt is concerned, nobody else matters. Just you. You are his *whole world.* And he runs and leaps and plays with you because he's happy. That's how he shows you his joy and his gratitude. For him, it's something just for the two of you to share. It's not for anyone else. And I want you to treasure that, because it's precious. You see, Annie, the problem isn't that other people can see *him*—it's that he can see other people, when all he wants to see is *you.*"

IN STITCHES

The drive home is quiet.

Annie is lost in her tumbling thoughts. Everything feels hopeless. All their training, all their potential—it won't amount to anything because she is no closer to a solution.

She sighs heavily. A moment later, his head on her lap, Runt sighs too.

They leave the blufflands behind them and return to the wide-open pastures. The sun is low in the sky. For a long straight stretch, beams of golden light are angled against the side of Bryan's face. He searches around the center console.

"Why can I never find my sunglasses?"

He squints, but it's still too bright. So he cups his palm and holds it against his temple, shielding his eyes from the sun so he can see directly ahead.

Annie looks over at him. Then she snaps her fingers.

She has an idea. One last sliver of hope.

Annie unfolds the map and turns it over to its blank side. She takes a pencil from her tool belt and begins sketching feverishly.

Bryan glances down and smiles.

"You're just like your grandpa," he murmurs.

It's dark when they arrive home.

Annie bursts into the farmhouse, full of urgency.

Susie and Dolly and Max look up at once.

"How did it go?" asks Susie.

"No good," Annie replies breathlessly, "but I think it's going to be okay. Do you still have your sewing machine?"

"Yes—it's at the back of the wardrobe somewhere. Why?"

Annie rushes to the table and spreads out the map.

Susie stands and looks over her sketches.

"Of course!" she exclaims. Then she claps her hands once, bringing them all to attention.

"Right. Not a moment to lose. Dolly, see if you can find a horse bridle from the old stable. Max, I need scissors and glue. Oh, and a hammer. Annie, keep that tool belt handy— I might need some bits and bobs."

Bryan shuffles into the room, yawning and scratching his chin, exhausted by the long day. He is surprised to find a hive of activity.

"What's going on here?"

"Ah," says Susie, "the man I want to see. Go and get your old leather jacket."

Bryan narrows his eyes. "Why?"

"It's being repurposed."

"But it's a classic!"

"Bryan, you haven't worn it in twenty years."

"And it still fits like a glove."

Susie gives him a doubtful look. But it's Annie's hopeful expression that persuades him to do as he's been asked.

Item after item is piled onto the table.

Finally, Susie plonks down a large sewing machine and wipes the dust off it. A strip of measuring tape hangs from her shoulder.

She takes a spool of thread from her sewing kit and gets started.

"Now, where's that doohickey? Gosh, I'm out of practice. Have we got everything?"

"I believe so," says Dolly.

"Wait, there's one thing missing. Where are you, Bryan?" Susie calls out.

Bryan speaks quietly from a distant room.

"I'm in here."

"What?" they all yell.

"I'm still in here!"

"Have you found the jacket?"

"Yes."

"Well, hurry up and bring it!"

There's a pause.

"I can't."

"Why not?" they all yell.

There's another pause.

Then Bryan enters the room. He has squeezed himself into a black leather jacket that is many sizes too small. His arms stick out sideways like a scarecrow's.

"I'm stuck," he says sheepishly.

His family stares at him for a moment. Then Dolly and Max collapse into howls of laughter. Bryan blushes.

Susie takes a deep, loving breath and walks over to Bryan.

"It must have shrunk with age," he explains.

Susie nods. "I'm sure that's the case."

"That's what happens with quality leather."

"Absolutely," Susie agrees.

She waves Annie over. Together they try to pull the jacket off.

"You're going to rip my arms off!" Bryan protests.

"How did you even get *into* this?"

Susie struggles, placing her foot on Bryan's back for leverage, as Annie tugs hard on a sleeve.

One last heave, and the jacket slips free. Bryan stumbles forward, and Susie and Annie tumble back. Everyone is on the floor. Runt tilts his head in confusion as the Shearers clamber to their feet. Bryan rubs his shoulder, though his pride has taken the most damage.

"Right," says Susie. "Let's get to work."

Over the next couple of hours, with Annie supervising and sketching and improving on her design, Susie measures, snips, sews, rips, glues, ties, hammers, tests, unpicks, clamps, and sews some more.

Finally, it's finished.

Susie holds it up.

"Best I can do. Let's give it a shot."

She hands it to Annie. It's a curious piece of equipment, with straps and buckles and a curved leather panel.

"What is it?" asks Max.

"I'll show you," says Annie.

She crouches in front of Runt and fits her invention snugly over his head. There are gaps in the straps for his ears to poke through, and she secures it by tightening the buckle under his chin. The leather panel stretches around his eyes like the brim of a bonnet, blocking his vision to the sides and the top so that Runt can see only what is directly in front of him, which happens to be Annie's face.

Runt rattles his head a couple of times.

"Ah, they're blinders," says Dolly. "Brilliant, Annie."

"Should we see if it works?" Susie asks.

The Shearers quietly creep out of Runt's view, their backs up against the wall. His ears twitch and swivel, following them.

Runt watches Annie retreat to the doorway.

She holds her breath.

Then she raises her magic finger.

And she points to her toes.

"Come on, Runt."

Runt doesn't move.

Susie crosses her fingers. Dolly prays. Max watches intently. Bryan urges Runt on, whispering to himself.

"Come on, it's okay," says Annie.

Runt dips his head, tentative, as though he is about to dive into cold water.

Annie bends down, filling his vision. "It's okay, come on."

Then, momentously, Runt takes a step. Then another. He walks all the way over to her.

Annie flicks her finger up, and Runt hops onto his hind legs, perfectly balanced. She guides him back down and draws circles in the air, spinning him around and around.

The Shearers applaud.

"It works!" Susie says, beaming.

"It's that quality leather," Bryan says. "Gives a man courage."

"Thank you," says Annie to everyone, but especially to Runt.

THE 97TH ANNUAL AUSTRALIAN CANINE AGILITY COURSE ASSOCIATION NATIONAL TITLES

The Shearers are running late.

Very late.

The whole family is crammed into their yellow sedan. Runt sits on Annie's lap in the back seat.

After a long morning on the road, they have reached the city. The streets are busy with traffic, and Bryan is getting flustered. He grips the steering wheel so tightly that his knuckles are white.

Calmly, Susie gives directions.

"Okay, you need to merge left and take the exit in two—"

"I can't merge if nobody will let me in!" Bryan interrupts. "Look at this! Is it against the law to let someone into a lane? Am I invisible?"

"Relax, you've got time," says Susie. "Take the exit in two—"

"There's no time! It's half past already!" Dolly calls from the back. "We're going to miss the competition!"

"Well, we would have got here sooner if I didn't have to pull over every twenty minutes, Mum!"

"My bladder's not what it used to be, Bryan! You'll see when you're older."

Susie tries yet again.

"So, ease left and take the exit in two—"

"I'm hungry," Max complains. "Isn't there *anything* to eat?"

Annie reaches into a pocket of her tool belt and pulls out a handful of almonds and raisins. She passes them across to Max.

"Oh. Thanks."

"Right!" Bryan exclaims. "That's it!"

He veers sharply into the lane beside him, causing a flurry of honking.

"Bryan, it's not—"

"Here we go!" says Bryan, who honks back as he takes an off-ramp and leaves the highway. He is pleased with himself.

"Bit of initiative," he says defiantly as he emerges onto a quieter road. "Sometimes you've got to take the bull by the horns. Show these city slickers what we're made of."

"Very impressive, dear," says Susie, "but you've taken the wrong exit."

"You said to take the exit!"

Susie patiently explains. "If anyone had let me finish my

sentence, you would have heard me say to take the exit *in two kilometers.*"

"Well! I . . ."

Bryan begins to protest but immediately realizes he is out of excuses.

"Everyone stop interrupting," he grumbles. "I need to concentrate. Now. Where am I? I'm lost."

After diligently following Susie's directions, Bryan brings the car to an abrupt stop outside the Australian Canine Agility Course Arena.

The Shearers bundle out and hurry toward the entrance.

Inside, Annie approaches a woman behind the administration desk.

"Excuse me, I'm Annie Shearer and this is Runt. I'm here for the agility course competition."

The clerk is a round woman with big hair. She is unimpressed.

"You're cutting it very close."

"That's my fault," Bryan volunteers.

"And mine," says Dolly.

"Is there anything to eat here?" asks Max, earning a clap to the back of the head from Susie.

The administration clerk looks over Annie's shoulder and shouts, making everyone flinch.

"Penny! This is your latecomer! Take her through!"

A volunteer approaches anxiously. She holds a clipboard tightly to her chest, as though she's worried somebody might steal it.

"*You're* Annie Shearer?"

"Yes."

"Oh, thank *goodness*! I've been looking everywhere for you. Gosh, you're very . . . well, you're very young, aren't you?"

"That going to be a problem?" asks Dolly, instinctively bunching her hands into fists.

"No, of course not," says Penny, wide-eyed. "I'm just surprised. You're also very late. You've missed the practice session, I'm afraid. Are you sure you still want to compete today?"

"Very much," says Annie.

"Okay, then you need to come with me immediately. The event is about to start."

Penny addresses the remaining Shearers.

"Beryl here will give you your tickets. You can enter through Gate A and find your seats."

"We can't go with Annie?" Bryan asks.

"Competitors only, I'm afraid."

"We'll be okay," Annie says.

"Knock 'em dead!" says Dolly.

Annie is about to follow Penny when Susie steps forward.

"Annie, wait!" she says urgently. "Don't forget these!"

She takes the blinders from her handbag.

"Oh, thank you," says Annie, relieved.

Susie smiles.

"We'll be cheering for both of you, but hopefully Runt won't notice."

Annie and Runt follow Penny down a long corridor, jogging to keep up with her brisk pace. Penny flicks through the pages on her clipboard as she walks.

"You're scheduled to run third, so let's get you straight out to the course. Now, your form doesn't seem to have a breed specified. What is he?"

"He's Runt," says Annie.

"Yes, I have his name recorded here. I need his breed."

"I don't know."

"Well, you must have his pedigree papers. What is the name of your registered kennel breeder?"

"I don't have one of those. Is it important?"

"Perhaps I should ask your parents."

"They don't know either. He was a stray."

Penny stops, stunned.

"He's a *stray* dog?"

"No," says Annie. "He *was* a stray dog. And now he lives with us. But where he came from doesn't matter."

The stadium has raised seating on two sides, and it's a packed crowd. The Shearers make their way up to the back row, apologizing as they shuffle past the other spectators.

They take their seats and look down at the bright green matting of the arena floor. The jumps and obstacles are clean and white. Bordering the course are purple banners advertising Mush Canine Cuisine. A referee wearing a black-and-white-striped shirt leans over the officials' desk. High on the wall is an electronic scoreboard.

"This is so proper," says Max.

"Of course it's proper. It's the National Titles!" says Bryan, as though he's been attending the event his whole life.

An announcer wearing a yellow pantsuit steps out into the middle of the arena with a microphone.

"Welcome, everyone, to the Ninety-Seventh Annual Australian Canine Agility Course Association National Titles!"

She smiles and pauses for applause.

"We have competitors from the very best kennels and training facilities from all over the country, so this year's will be a tight contest! We're just about ready to get under way, so I'll invite our first team onto the floor. It's Sharon Sprout and her Hungarian pointer, Poprock!"

Annie watches from a waiting area beside the stands. She hears the crowd warmly applauding as Sharon and Poprock run past and onto the floor.

She kneels to fit and adjust Runt's blinders.

"You'll be okay, Runt. Look, see? It's just me. There's nobody else but us. We can do this. It's just like at home. You and me."

Surreptitiously peering at her from around the corner of a nearby hallway is Fergus Fink. He is dressed in a gold-sequined tracksuit with purple tassels. Simpkins stands behind, holding a crate with Chariot inside.

Fergus turns with a diabolical smile.

"Simpkins, fetch me a copy of the Official Canine Code. Forthwith! Toot sweet!"

He narrows his eyes at Annie Shearer and whispers to himself. "I've got her."

A SPANNER IN THE WORKS

Perched on the edges of their seats, the Shearers watch Poprock blitz the course, dashing and skipping and leaping and flashing across the finishing line. The referee holds up a green paddle to the officials' desk, giving Poprock the all clear. A moment later, Poprock's name and time appear on the scoreboard.

"41.39 seconds," says Bryan. "That's impressive."

Dolly scoffs and waves it off. "Please!" she says loudly, her competitive juices flowing again for the first time in years. "We'll beat that easy!"

Susie leans across. "Just calm yourselves down, you two. We're not at the football."

The announcer steps out with a smile.

"We're off to a flying start, but there are some big names to come. Next to the floor we have Horace Schmick and his boxer, Peanut!"

The crowd puts their hands together.

Max, who has been filming since he sat down, has allowed his daredevil eyes to wander. Head tilted back, he stares longingly at the high scaffolding under the roof.

Susie is quick to notice, and she whispers into his ear. "Don't even think about it, or your whole body will need a plaster cast—and it won't be due to misadventure."

Sullenly, Max nods and points his camera back at the action.

Annie watches closely as Horace and Peanut work their way around the course. At one point, Peanut tips the bar of the high jump and it clatters to the ground. The referee holds up a red paddle. The crowd groans in sympathy, understanding that it means a time penalty.

Horace looks disappointed when they finish. He gives Peanut a comforting pat, but Peanut really doesn't care.

Annie is up next. She waits nervously for her name to be called.

Behind her, in the shadows of the hallway, Simpkins returns with a hefty leather-bound book.

"What took you so long?" Fergus hisses as he snatches it. He turns the pages hurriedly.

Horace and Peanut walk past Annie as the announcer steps onto the floor.

"I'm really excited about these next two, folks. All the way from Upson Downs, our youngest ever handler by some margin, we have Annie Shearer and her"—the announcer frowns at the competitor card, looking for Runt's breed—"*dog . . .* Runt!"

Annie takes a deep breath and walks out with Runt by her side. She squints. The lights are brighter than she expected. She can feel everyone staring down at her. For a moment, it is still and tense; then the applause hits her like a gust of wind.

Runt keeps his head low, his vision shielded by the blinders.

In the back row, the Shearers all stand and cheer. Bryan points and grins, deliriously proud.

"There she is!"

He excitedly nudges the spectator beside him, who clutches a bucket of popcorn on his lap protectively.

"That's my daughter! And that's our Runt! Look at her! Go, Annie!"

Susie claps and hollers. She already has tears in her eyes.

Dolly is fired up. She shakes her fists. "Give it a rip, love!"

On the floor, the announcer gives Annie a friendly smile. "Good luck!"

The referee points Annie toward the starting line, and Annie leads Runt over. She crouches, lifts his head, and looks him in the eyes.

"Remember, it's just like at home. Don't worry about all the sheep outside the fence—just keep looking at me. You can do it. If we win this, we can go to London and try to pay the overdraft on the overdraft, and then I'll be able to afford all the Mush you could ever eat."

The referee calls out. "Take your position, please!"

Annie holds up her magic finger, bidding Runt to stay.

She walks backward. Runt shifts his weight forward, but he remains behind the line.

Annie stands in the middle of the course and looks around, taking careful note of every obstacle, imagining the exact path they will take.

She turns and looks at Runt.

Her heart pounds.

The crowd is silent.

Her magic finger quivers.

"Halt!"

A voice bellows from beyond the course.

"Stop the competition!"

The crowd gasps and murmurs in confusion.

A moment later, Fergus Fink storms into view, holding up a sheet of paper torn from the Official Canine Code. He snatches the microphone from the announcer and strides into the middle of the floor.

"A great transgression is afoot, ladies and gentlemen! Fraudulence! Treachery! Don't be fooled by the innocent appearance of this young conspirator. A cheating scandal is unfolding right before your eyes, and *around* the eyes of this wicked little creature."

He points accusingly at Runt.

The Shearers are confused.

Dolly is bemused.

"Who is this glittering parrot?"

Fergus continues.

"It's all here in the Official Canine Code. Clause six, subsection two: *No leashes or material aids may be employed between handler and canine.* And behold! This animal is employing outlawed equipment, resulting in an unfair advantage. The evidence is incontrovertible! Incontestable! *Irrefutable!* I move for an immediate disqualification and a lifetime ban from our hallowed institution! As a Fink, and a fighter for fairness, I consider this the darkest day in our storied history. Thank goodness there was a hero among us brave enough to prevent such a grave injustice!"

Bryan is outraged.

"What is he on about?"

He throws his hands up, inadvertently hitting the tub of popcorn on the lap of his neighbor. The bucket flies into the air, causing an explosion of popcorn.

The only person happy about this is Max, who scavenges like a greedy squirrel, stuffing popcorn into his cheeks before Susie can slap his hands away.

On the arena floor, Annie stands all alone.

She watches the referee in serious discussion with the officials at the desk. They take turns speaking into a black telephone. Fergus Fink and the announcer stand nearby. Penny also approaches the desk, looking concerned.

Annie is embarrassed and unsure of what to do. She didn't know that Runt's blinders might be considered against the rules. Every pair of eyes in the stadium is fixed on her, and she feels herself shrinking. She wishes she could call Runt over, because everything is always better when he is by her side.

Finally, Penny walks over to Annie, still clutching her clipboard.

"I'm sorry, Annie—you'll have to come with me."

"But it's our turn!"

Penny leads Annie toward a set of double doors on the opposite side of the course. Runt follows them.

The announcer has wrested the microphone back from Fergus Fink.

"Apologies for the interruption, everyone. A competitor's complaint has been deemed credible, so an immediate inquiry has been launched. Our protocols dictate that Annie and Runt are subject to a board review."

The crowd is restless now. They begin booing loudly, and Annie suspects it is directed at her. So too does Fergus, who nods smugly to himself.

It's not until Annie has exited through the double doors that it becomes clear the crowd is on her side.

"Let her run!" someone yells.

"Get on with it!"

"Give the girl a go!"

In the back row, the Shearers are incensed.

"Get it together, ref!" yells Max.

Bryan and Dolly are ready to charge down the steps, but Susie, as always, is poised and calm. She urges them to sit down.

"Just wait and see what happens."

THE TRIAL

Annie's footsteps echo down a dark passageway. The noise of the stadium has been drowned out.

"Where are we going?" she asks nervously.

"Not too much farther," says Penny.

"Am I in trouble?"

Penny doesn't respond.

They stop outside a door with a painted label that reads: **AUSTRALIAN CANINE AGILITY COURSE ASSOCIATION BOARDROOM.**

It creaks open and Penny ushers Annie inside.

The air is thick and stale, as though it hasn't left the room in a hundred years. The carpet is musty and moss green. The walls feature wooden plaques with the names of past winners written in gold. Elsewhere there are black-and-white photographs of previous National Titles and painted portraits of the association founders standing proudly beside their dogs.

At the far end of the room, four members of the board sit behind a long desk. Their names are engraved on brass plates in front of them. There is an empty seat on the far right end.

Penny strips a page from her clipboard and hands it to a stern old man in the middle. His name is Ron Ronalds, and he is the chair of the board. He has thin silver hair and wears a tweed suit and a brown tie.

Penny bows and backs out of the room, closing the door behind her.

Despite wearing thick spectacles, Ron Ronalds takes out a magnifying glass from inside his jacket and uses it to read the page Penny has handed him. Everyone waits for him in respectful silence.

Annie stands with her hands behind her back.

Runt sits and sniffs her ankles.

Finally, Ron clears his throat. He squints hard at Runt for almost a full minute.

"Young lady, could you explain the nature of the accessory fitted to your companion?"

"It's so that he can't see anybody but me. Otherwise he won't move. It doesn't make him go faster or anything. I don't even know if it works yet."

Ron nods slowly.

The board huddles together, and they speak in low whispers. Annie has to strain to hear their conversation.

"Well, they're widely used in horse racing. I don't see how they—"

"Jockeys use whips too, Geraldine. Do you propose we permit those?"

"My interpretation of the law is that it strictly refers to leashes."

"Or any material aid, which this clearly is!"

"The question is, Does narrowing the dog's vision result in a competitive advantage?"

"Of course it does! It reduces potential distraction. It also—"

"But it hinders the field of view, which is a clear *disadvantage.*"

"A dog must be responsible for its own focus and discipline."

Ron Ronalds bangs a gavel shaped like a bone. Annie flinches.

"Enough!" he declares. "The board must come to order. Votes must be cast. Mrs. Chauncey, what say you?"

"Permitted," says Mrs. Chauncey.

"And you, Mr. Maggs?"

"Denied and duly disqualified," says Mr. Maggs, who, it must be said, is a pompous and persnickety man.

Ron Ronalds turns to his left.

"Mr. Pitts?"

"Permitted," says Mr. Pitts.

Ron Ronalds nods slowly.

Annie watches him, hope rising in her chest.

"As for my determination: After considering the facts as

they relate to my interpretation of the code, my opinion is to deny the use of this apparatus. Its application, in my view, constitutes a disqualifying act. However, removing the offending device *would* permit you the opportunity to run and record a time."

Annie is struggling to keep up. The more he speaks, the less she understands.

"Does this mean we can still have our turn?" she asks.

"Yes. And no. You see, at two votes apiece, we are, it seems, at an impasse."

"A what?" Annie asks.

"A draw," says Mrs. Chauncey.

"A dead heat," says Mr. Maggs.

"A tie," says Mr. Pitts.

Together, they all turn their heads like clowns in a carnival game, looking at the empty chair at the end of the desk.

"Hasn't cast a vote in over eight years," sighs Mr. Pitts, shaking his head.

"A real shame," says Mrs. Chauncey.

Ron Ronalds lifts his gavel again.

"Since our colleague is absent and cannot cast a vote, it seems you are neither permitted nor denied the right to race. So I'm afraid that this means you will be unable to—"

Behind Annie, the door swings open.

She turns to see Bernadette Box defiantly enter the room.

"Get your hand off your gavel, Ron."

The board members gasp. They are too shocked to speak.

Bernadette gives Annie a little wink. Then she bustles across the room and takes her rightful seat as the fifth and deciding board member. She tucks her chair in.

"Permitted."

Then she reaches across, snatches Ron's gavel, bangs it, nods, and smiles.

"Go get 'em, Annie."

HERE COMES ANNIE

The Shearers have all but lost hope.

Bryan slumps in his seat, arms folded. Dolly scowls, Max sulks, and Susie frowns. None of them knows where Annie has been taken.

A schnauzer bounds across the finishing line. The Shearers are too disappointed to join in the applause. The man next to Bryan munches on a fresh tub of popcorn.

The announcer steps onto the course.

"Give a hand to Frances O'Brien and Kit! Well done. A solid effort. Folks, that was our last scheduled competitor. . . ."

"What a joke," Bryan says. "Should we go find Annie?"

"Worst of all," says Dolly, "that twinkling clown has won. Look."

She points to the electronic scoreboard. Sure enough, with a time of 38.86 seconds, Fergus Fink is in the lead. He has a clear advantage over the rest of the field.

After years being runner-up, he has finally finished first.

Fergus waits by the side of the course, smirking as the announcer speaks, waiting impatiently to be declared champion.

"Which means, of course, that our winner this year is—"

The announcer stops abruptly and turns around. She is beckoned over to the officials' desk and handed the black telephone. She listens, nods, and hangs up.

"Stay in your seats, folks, because I have good news. It's not over yet! I've just been informed that the board has made their decision, and Annie Shearer and Runt have been cleared to run!"

The crowd cheers.

Susie smiles. "Oh, thank goodness!"

"There she is!" Max points.

The double doors swing open and Annie and Runt step into the arena. The audience grows even louder.

Fergus Fink is livid. He stomps over to the referee to appeal, but he is waved away.

"And here is Annie now!" says the announcer. "This will certainly be our last run of the day, and 38.86 seconds is the benchmark. But a reminder that our top two finishers both earn an invitation to compete next month at the Krumpet's Dog Show in London, where they will vie for the grand prize of a quarter of a million dollars."

"*What?*" the Shearers all say at once.

Bryan's mouth and eyes are wide open.

"Did she just say . . . ?"

"A quarter of a million dollars," Dolly confirms.

"That's a lot of cheddar," says Max.

"So *that's* why Annie has been working so hard at this," Susie says softly to herself.

With her chest full of pride, she watches Annie cross the arena floor and sit Runt down behind the white starting line for the second time.

Annie kneels. She scratches his chin and gives him a comforting rub.

"I'm right here. Don't worry about anyone else. It's the same as before, Runt. This is our chance. Just follow me and do your best. We can beat his time."

The crowd grows quiet as Annie resumes her position in the middle of the course.

The Shearers are frozen with nerves.

Bryan's fingers are tightly crossed.

"Please run, Runt. Come on, mate."

An official at the desk nods to the referee, who nods back.

Annie takes a deep breath.

She lifts her magic finger and waits for the three chimes.

Three . . . two . . . one . . .

"*Go! Go! Go!* Come on, Runt!"

Runt blasts into motion, like he's been fired out of a cannon.

"*Yes!*" yells Susie, waving her fist.

Runt is flying. Annie is exhilarated, weaving him neatly

through the slaloms, up and over the balance beam, through the hoop jump, and into the first tunnel.

The crowd urges them on, louder and louder. Runt hops up the seesaw, teeters patiently, then dashes down, soars over the hurdle, and turns back to take the tunnel again. Annie guides him expertly, calling instructions and tracing a path with her magic finger.

Dolly twitches and jerks on the edge of her seat, as though she's out there running the course with them.

Max films with shaking hands.

Bryan is completely frozen, holding his breath. Unblinking.

Runt leaps over the long jump and takes one final sprint for the line.

He finishes the course. Then he spins and sits, looking up at Annie, ready to go again.

Annie is exhausted. Her heart pounds.

The crowd applauds wildly; then they murmur among themselves about the possibility that Annie and Runt might have achieved the impossible. An expectant hush falls over the stadium.

The referee holds up his green paddle to the officials' desk.

All clear.

Everyone stares at the scoreboard.

Except Susie, who can't bear to look.

Bernadette Box peeks through a gap in the doors on the other side of the arena.

"Come on, Annie," she whispers.

Fergus Fink glares at the screen.

Annie smiles down at Runt, because she already knows.

The time flashes up beside their names.

38.78 seconds.

Annie and Runt have *won*.

The crowd roars. They are thrilled and delighted. Annie blushes. Runt looks up at her.

"Good job, Runt. We did it."

Annie holds out a triumphant fist, and Runt bumps her knuckles with his paw.

Bryan leaps to his feet, pumping his arms. Once again, he has upended the popcorn of his neighbor, sending a confetti of puffy kernels into the air. The Shearers hug and dance and yell. Max, mildly suffocated by the exuberant embrace of his family, pans across the crowd with his camera.

Fergus Fink is in a fit of fury. Simpkins quietly retreats with Chariot, knowing better than to be in the path of his tirade. Fergus storms over to the officials' desk and thumps it with both hands.

"No!" he tantrums. "No! No! No! No! No! No! *I* won! I *won*! This is a violation of the rules! A clear contravention of the code! I *won*!"

But nobody is listening. Everyone is simply too happy for Annie and Runt.

Bernadette Box brings her hands to her mouth, covering her grin. Then she slips away quietly, back down the corridor.

The announcer leads Annie and Runt to the center of the arena. She hands Annie a big glass trophy, an envelope, and a novelty check for one thousand dollars.

Volunteers, sponsors, the other competitors, and their dogs have all stepped out to show their support. They stand nearby and smile. Photographers close in.

Uneasy and shy, Annie and Runt back away.

"Come back, Annie! We're not finished with you yet!" says the announcer. "Congratulations to you and Runt, our new national champions!"

The crowd commends their achievement.

"What an amazing story. Our youngest handler, and now our youngest ever winner. Annie, how are you feeling?"

"Oh . . ." Annie struggles to find the words. "I don't know. Pretty good, I suppose."

Runt is agitated. It's loud and crowded, and the flashing of the camera disturbs him. He hides behind Annie and rattles his head. He paws at his blinders, and they come loose. He lifts his head to see a stadium full of people and dogs, all focused on him.

He backs up, overwhelmed. His old instincts are triggered.

He bolts for the corridor and vanishes.

Dogs bark and pull on their handlers' leashes, wanting to chase him, causing a tangle in the middle of the arena.

Annie drops everything—her trophy, her envelope, her check—and goes after Runt, sprinting the length of the floor and disappearing through the double doors.

In the back row, the Shearers watch it all unfold. Worried, they quickly file out together, hustling urgently down the steps.

THE DEVIL IN THE DETAILS

They find Annie and Runt sitting under a tree in a nearby park.

"Thank goodness we found you!" says Susie. "Is everything all right?"

Susie carries the blinders, Max has the trophy, Bryan holds the big check, and Dolly clutches the envelope.

"He's better now," says Annie.

"Annie, you won! Look!"

Bryan holds out the big check, but Annie doesn't take it.

"It's okay—you keep it," she says.

"Runt was like lightning out there!" says Susie.

"When do we all go to London?" asks Max.

"I don't think any of us are going," Dolly says.

Her tone is serious. The others turn to look at her. Dolly has opened the envelope and is reading the fine print of the document inside. She has to squint and hold it at arm's length because she has forgotten her reading glasses.

"What do you mean?" asks Bryan. "They said she won an invitation to the Krumpet's Dog Show in London."

"She *has,* but . . ."

"Is something wrong?" Annie asks.

Bryan takes the document from Dolly. He quickly mumbles as he scans the page.

". . . *wish to congratulate you* . . . yes, yes, yes . . . *cordially extend an invitation* . . . yes, yes, yes . . ."

"Farther down," says Dolly.

". . . *be advised that all flights and travel expenses, accommodations, entrant fees, insurance agreements, ancillary costs, and any potential fiscal liabilities arising from your participation not herein described are at the sole discretion of the competitor.*"

"What does that mean?" asks Annie.

"It means we can't afford to go, love," says Susie softly.

"I'm so sorry, mate," says Bryan, and he really is. The puff has gone out of his chest. In fact, everyone seems to deflate together.

"But . . . we can win it," Annie says.

"I don't doubt for a second that you could," Bryan replies. "But even with a check this big, it's just too expensive."

Annie looks across to Susie, and she can see from her mother's expression that she agrees.

And just like that, it is all over.

At sunset, back at the farm, with the sheep watching curiously from the fence line, Annie takes her obstacle course apart. She pulls up the stumps, stacks the planks, and dismantles the jumps. She won't be needing any of them anymore.

Runt helps too, dragging bits and pieces over to the pile.

Bryan opens the gate and steps into the practice paddock.

"You want some help?"

Annie shrugs as she rolls the motorcycle tire along the ground.

"Is the big check enough to pay the overdraft on the overdraft?" she asks.

Bryan rubs his chest, because Annie has a way of making his heart swell up so large that it feels like it might burst.

"Annie, listen. You don't have to try to fix everything. The most important thing to me is that you're happy."

Annie lets the tire wobble and fall.

"But fixing things makes me happy."

Bryan chuckles to himself. He can't argue with that.

He looks over at Runt.

"Mate, I know you don't listen to a word I say, but you're a special dog, and you were amazing today. You both were. And we're all very proud. You know, I overheard a lady in the crowd say that your time would have given them a run for their money over there in London. Think of that, eh?"

They go quiet, reflecting on what might have been.

"Anyway, I'll leave you to it." Bryan clears his throat and trudges off, closing the gate behind him.

Annie looks down and notices she is standing in the long shadow of the Rainmaker. It is completely still, like a frozen Ferris wheel. There is no wind, no clouds, no rain, no hope. As hard as she tries, nothing seems to work.

Nearby, she sees the shrunken balloon head of a scarecrow grinning at her. She feels mocked by it. With one great, frustrated shove, Annie pushes it over. It feels satisfying. In a rush of anger, she pushes over the tailor's dummy, then the mannequins, and she tears down all the other members of the crowd.

The moment she is done, she feels guilty. She picks up the tailor's dummy and brushes the dust from it.

"Sorry, everyone," she says.

DOLLY THE DODGER

It's almost dark when Runt sits patiently beside his food bowl, looking up at his two favorite things in the world: Annie Shearer and a fresh tin of Mush Canine Cuisine.

Annie cracks the can and tears off the lid. She tips it upside down, and the tube slides and splats. Runt dives in.

Dolly leans on the corner of the farmhouse, watching.

"He really loves that stuff, doesn't he?"

"It's all he ever wants to eat," says Annie.

"Well, he earned it today," says Dolly. Then she waves Annie over. "Come with me—I want to show you something."

Annie follows Dolly through the house and into her bedroom. Dolly's shelves are packed with shiny trophies and medallions and ribbons and sashes and team photos. Right in the middle, Annie recognizes the silver cup she won at the Woolarama Show and her glass National Title trophy from earlier that day.

Dolly points at them.

"I found these next to the bins outside."

"I don't need them," Annie says.

"Why?"

"Because they don't fix anything."

Dolly looks at Annie and thinks for a moment.

Then she rummages through an old chest and emerges with a worn pair of leather boxing gloves.

"Hold out your hands."

Dolly slips the gloves onto Annie's hands and laces them up.

"How do they feel?"

"They're a bit big," says Annie.

"I think they fit you just fine."

Dolly holds her palms up.

"Righto—give 'em a whack, hard as you can."

Annie gives a couple of tentative prods.

"Come on," says Dolly. "You're not gonna hurt me."

Annie swings harder. Most jabs miss their mark, but a few smack into the meat of Dolly's hands.

"That's it! Good! How's that? Feel better?"

"A little bit, I suppose. It's fun."

"Let me tell you a story," says Dolly. "I grew up with five brothers, so I knew my way around a scrap. Nothing delighted me more than putting those boys back in their place. When I got a bit older, my brother Ted, your great-uncle, he had designs on being a boxer. He needed someone to spar with, so we trained in the backyard together for hours and hours. He didn't hold back, and neither did I. Ted was a bit of a brawler, really. No footwork, but he had a lot of heart. I went to every fight of his, cheered him on. He was moving up the ranks, but then he met Marilyn Foxtrot, and suddenly he had other things on his mind. But I was hooked, you see. And I wanted to get out there. Now, Ted had an amateur flyweight bout coming up that he completely forgot about. So I went to a barber and got my hair cut short. I drew myself a little mustache just like Ted's with an eyeliner pencil. And I nicked his trunks and his singlet and those gloves you've got on now, and I went to fight in his name."

"You *really* did that?"

"Too right I did."

"Were you scared?"

"Petrified! This was a rough crowd. The fight was held in an old fish-canning factory by the docks. To this day, if I get a whiff of salmon, I go wobbly at the knees."

"What happened?"

"Well, I wore his robe with the hood right up over my head until the bell sounded to start the first round. Lucky for me, the lighting wasn't very good in there. So the fight gets going, and my opponent can't lay a glove on me. I clock his chin with a couple of counterjabs, and that's what got people suspicious, you see. Ted was a first-round cyclone, but I was a very different fighter. Then, by the end of the second round, my mustache had rubbed off and the jig was up. They stopped the fight."

"Did you get in trouble?"

"Oh, it was quite a scandal. Most of the crowd thought it was a big joke. But my opponent's team was furious because I was winning the fight. So I had to scamper out of there, quick smart. Still had those gloves on when I got home. But the next day, a promoter by the name of Billy Southpaw came to the house. He walked straight past Ted and said he wanted to train me and take me on the road. He managed a crew of boxers and rodeo stars who toured around country carnivals and cattle musters. He'd set up a ring under a big marquee and challenge the locals to go three rounds against his best fighters. He had been on the lookout for someone like me, because the ladies always complained that they wanted a shot in the ring too."

"Did you go?"

"Of course! I was away for years, went all around the country. And every new town I visited, the response was the same. They laughed at me, they heckled, and they made fun. They booed and scoffed and carried on. They were trying to make me feel weak, but they only made me stronger. They made me determined to prove them wrong. Because nobody *ever* has the right to make you feel small. As soon as that bell sounded and they saw me fight, I earned their respect. I never lost a single bout. And within a year, I was the main event. Dolly the Dodger, they called me. But even so, every weekend, every new place, I had to earn their respect all over again. Now, can you guess why I wanted to tell you that story?"

"No."

"Because when I saw you out there today, it was like going back in time. You stood your ground. The odds were against you, but you didn't give up. Life is just like that obstacle course. There are *always* hoops to jump through, and *always* long tunnels where you can't quite see the light at the end. So don't give up now, Annie. We will find a way, and we will do it together. Keep swinging, keep fighting. We'll get you to London, and they won't know what's hit them."

Dolly holds her palms up. Annie smiles and batters her hands with another flurry of punches.

"That's the spirit," says Dolly.

THE CHERISHED RASCAL

Long after Annie is asleep, Bryan and Susie sit at the dinner table.

With her right hand, Susie taps numbers into the old adding machine. With her left hand, she searches the internet for cheap flights and accommodations.

The kettle boils. Bryan gets up, then returns with two cups of tea.

"Forget it, Susie. We can't make it work."

Susie holds up a finger, concentrating. She finishes a couple of sums on the machine, then rips off the paper ribbon.

"There's a chance," she says. "If we lock in the right package, we might just have enough for you and Annie and Runt to get to London."

Bryan isn't convinced.

"That sounds terrific—but we've still got a mountain of

bills here, with more on the way. And we've still got Robert-Barren breathing down our necks. Besides, I can't leave the farm—there's so much to—"

Susie reaches out and puts her hand over his.

"Bryan, you haven't had a break in over ten years. You should go."

"But how are we going to raise the money to get there?"

Dolly suddenly appears in the doorway.

"We'll do what we have to," she says.

Dolly steps forward. She places two gold wedding rings on the table.

One belonged to Wally.

The other one is hers.

"Mum, no, you can't," says Bryan.

"They're no use to me now," says Dolly. "And it's what Wally would want. You know, he worked a whole summer at the brickworks to afford these. I thought he'd been going to the pub. These two rings are about love. And family. And sacrifice. That's why it's the right thing to do. We'll get decent money for them. Won't be enough for the whole trip, but it's a start."

Bryan knows better than to argue.

Susie is suddenly inspired. "I can bake some more pies!"

Bryan and Dolly speak over each other.

"Oh, you don't need to do that."

"That's really not necessary."

"Nonsense!" Susie chirps. "Every bit helps, and they were a big hit at the Woolarama Show."

Again, Bryan knows better than to argue.

He picks up the ribbon of numbers from the adding machine and raises his eyebrows.

"You know, we might just scrape up enough."

"Don't tell Annie yet," Susie whispers. "We'll surprise her."

It's a sunny Saturday in Upson Downs.

Susie Shearer wears a blue blouse with orange polka dots, pink high-waisted flared trousers, big brass hoop earrings, a yellow beaded necklace, and a green silk headscarf as she steps onto the main street to take pie orders.

Susie doesn't have to walk far. By now, the locals have all heard about Runt and Annie winning at the National Titles, and they are all eager to show their support.

It seems everyone wants to help Susie Shearer raise the funds to get to London, but what they *don't* want are her pies. The reasons they give are quite odd, almost as though they are going out of their way to avoid them.

"No pies for me, no . . . I'm . . . allergic," says Jan Fancy.

"You're specifically allergic to pies?" asks Susie.

"Yes. I come out in a horrific rash. It's very strange."

"What about tarts?" Susie asks.

Jan thinks for a moment. "Do you make tarts?"

"Sure, I can make tarts."

"What a shame. I'm allergic to them too. But here's twenty dollars all the same. Good luck!"

She hurries away, leaving Susie feeling both grateful and confused.

Most curious of all is the town's change of heart when it comes to Runt. He is no longer a stray nuisance. He's a lovable scoundrel. A cherished rascal. A treasured part of the community. It's as though they have entirely rewritten Runt's history, and they now take a proud ownership over his achievements.

"Caught him in my tomato bushes a few summers back," says Bruce Darrow with misty eyes. "He was off like a bullet, cleared the back fence easy as you like. He was always an extraordinary dog, that's for sure. Here's fifty dollars—all the best to you."

"Thank you," says Susie.

"We heard you were raising some money to get our little Runt overseas, so we've passed the hat around," says Mervyn Froth, the publican at the Golden Fleece. "We always knew he was headed for something special, the cheeky little blighter."

Susie raises a skeptical eyebrow.

"Is that so?" she asks.

"Oh, my oath. Credit to your Annie, of course, for reining him in. And to you, for giving him a home and whatnot. Anyway, here's a hundred dollars."

"Thank you," says Susie.

All day, people approach Susie and make modest contributions. Annie's teacher, Ms. Formsby, gives Susie an envelope of money and a card saying *Good Luck, Annie,* which has been signed by everyone in her class.

"They've all donated their pocket money," says Ms. Formsby. "And the staff has chipped in too."

"Thank you," says Susie.

The only person who hasn't changed their opinion is Runt's old nemesis, Constable Duncan Bayleaf, who scoffs as he walks by.

"I see my efforts in trying to capture that bag of fleas have turned him into quite an athlete. You're welcome. Though I don't suppose any gratitude will come my way. Far as I'm concerned, if you've got any sense, you'll leave that mutt over there. He's nothing but trouble."

"Thank you, Constable," Susie says, then rolls her eyes as soon as his back is turned.

The exchange doesn't dampen her spirits. Over the course of the day, Susie doesn't sell a single pie, but she raises more money than she could have dreamed.

WALLY'S WORDS OF WISDOM

While Susie is away in town, Annie has been trying to think of ways to get to London, but she is hopelessly stuck.

In search of answers, she goes to the shearing shed and stands at Wally's workbench. She thumbs through his sketchbooks, combing through his mad inventions for something potentially lucrative.

She uncovers pages of designs for an automatic shearing machine. It looks like a giant mechanical spider, full of pulleys and levers and spindly arms with clippers at the end.

Another fanciful project is a method for sheep to grow colorful wool so their fleece won't have to be dyed. Wally proposed adding bright pigments to their food. According to his research, if people ate too many carrots, their skin turned orange. Likewise, the reason flamingos were pink was because of the shrimp in their diet.

Annie looks at Runt, who has hopped up onto the bench.

"Maybe your fur is brown because all you eat is Mush," she says.

Another book of ingenious schemes is dedicated to water.

Wally was developing ways to remove the salt from seawater to make the ocean drinkable, but it's all much too complicated for Annie to understand.

She pores over sketches of a huge machine he called the Fogsucker. It appears to be a giant vacuum cleaner attached to a tractor, with large tubes poking from the sides to inhale fog on cold mornings, collecting the vapor in a big tank.

Annie thinks it's a brilliant idea, but she couldn't even begin to build it in time. She closes the book. None of Wally's wild notions are going to help them get to London.

As she shelves the sketchbook, she notices a small leather-bound journal that must have slipped behind the other books. She pulls it out, blows away the dust, and opens it. She has never seen it before. It's filled with Wally's small scratchy handwriting, but there are no pictures or diagrams.

She looks closer and notices it's Wally's diary.

Annie feels a guilty knot in her stomach. She suspects that she shouldn't be reading it.

But for reasons she doesn't quite understand, she feels a strong urge to flick through the pages, all the way to the end.

She reads the very last entry:

It's been a year now since Bryan came back to help with the farm while I prepare our case against Earl Robert-Barren. We can't afford the lawyers anymore, so I've been studying up to argue in court myself. I've a fighting chance if we get a judge with his head screwed on right. Dolly says I'll need a suit. Susie reckons she can make one cheap with that machine of hers.

I'm worried about the town if the case doesn't go our way. If that monster keeps hoarding water, the whole district will dry out and die, and there won't be any of us left. There's already talk of people selling up. I've never seen the river this low at this time of year. The weather is changing too, I swear it.

Still, there's a fair bit to be thankful for, now that I put pen to paper and think on it. It's nice to have everyone here under the same roof. If I have any regrets, it's that I haven't spent more time with the people I've tried to provide for. I'm solitary by nature, I suppose. Such is the life of a shepherd.

Max is three now and a real tearaway. I caught him trying to jump off the roof of the chicken coop yesterday. I gave him a few stern words, but back he went an hour later.

Annie is only one year old, but she's my little mate. She can't speak yet, and Lord knows I'm not a chatterbox, but we understand each other. She loves to be here in the shed with me. As I write this, she's sitting on the bench, playing with the pockets of my tool belt. She's fascinated by it. She's a thinker and a fixer—I can tell that already. And she's a natural with animals. One day I reckon she'll do great things.

I'm happy they're all here. It's nice to have a full house. Susie is like a walking rainbow. She brightens every room, which is just what we need right now.

I'm grateful for Bryan's help. He works hard and he does his best, but he doesn't have an instinct for it. His head is elsewhere. I know he has passions he'd prefer to follow more than my footsteps, and I hope that once I get our water back, he will go out and explore them. He feels it's his duty to be here. And the truth is, I couldn't take on Earl if Bryan wasn't holding the fort. He's a good man and a good son, but he deserves to walk his own path. Everyone does.

Annie closes the diary.

Reading Grandpa Wally's words gives her a strange sensation. She feels empty and full at the same time. Happy and sad.

She wishes she could remember sitting on the bench with him while he wrote it. Runt is lying in the same spot where she would have been. Annie reaches out and gives him a rub behind the ears.

Annie tears the last entry from the diary. She folds it up neatly and puts it in a pocket of her tool belt.

She may not have found a way to make money, but she knows she has discovered something very valuable.

Just as Annie carefully removes the page from the diary, Bryan carefully removes a tarpaulin from the back of his truck.

He is parked in the delivery bay behind Patel's Petals, the only florist in Upson Downs.

Standing nearby, Gretel Patel gasps when Bryan reveals a colorful selection of potted plants taken from his greenhouse. Most impressive among them, of course, is his award-winning rainbow rose.

"It's you!" Gretel declares. "*You* are the enigmatic genius!"

Bryan blushes and looks down at his feet. He clears his throat.

"Well . . . I don't know about *genius*."

Giddy, Gretel comes forward, looking over Bryan's plants with awe and wonder.

"What type of rose is this?" She points to a big purple-and-white flower sprouting from the end of a single stalk. The petals are firm and thick.

"Ah. I'm very proud of this one. It's not a rose, though."

"It's not?"

"No."

"What is it?"

Bryan smiles.

"It's a cabbage."

"A cabbage?"

"A cabbage. See, it's a beautiful ornamental. Gorgeous color. But it's good eating too. Not too bitter. Very crisp and sweet. You can whack it into a stew or toss it into a salad. Try it."

Gretel snaps off a petal and takes a crunchy munch. Her eyes go wide.

"Incredible! *Delicious!* You are a marvel. A true innovator! And look at these extraordinary specimens. What is this flower? It looks like . . ."

"A miniature magnolia, that's right."

"They smell *divine,* Mr. Shearer."

"Please. Call me Bryan."

Gretel turns, quivering with excitement.

"Bryan, I must have these magnificent creations. The world *must* see them."

"Gretel," says Bryan, folding his arms and leaning on the truck, "make me an offer."

WOLF AT THE DOOR

That night, Susie's fingers dance like a concert pianist's as she taps numbers into the adding machine. Laid out in neat stacks are the donations she collected during the day.

Dolly enters the dining room carrying her velvet purse. She takes out the money she earned from selling her wedding rings and puts it on the table.

Susie stops counting. She places her hand on her heart and looks up at Dolly, overcome with emotion.

"Oh, shoosh," says Dolly. "Don't you start. They're just bits of metal. Have we got enough yet?"

Susie counts Dolly's notes and adds that sum to the total. Her shoulders slump and she puts her head in her hands.

"Not quite," she says. "But we're *so* close."

Max pipes up.

"I could sell my camera," he says. "Might get a bit for it."

"No, love, you don't need to do that."

"No, you certainly don't," says Bryan, striding into the room triumphantly.

Max, Dolly, and Susie watch quizzically as he digs his hand deep into his back pocket.

"What *are* you doing?" Dolly asks.

After considerable fumbling, Bryan plucks out a fat wad of cash and slaps it on the table.

The other three stare at it, stunned.

"Where did you get all that?" Susie asks.

"Robbed a bank," says Bryan.

"Did you really?" Max asks, excited.

Bryan lowers his eyebrows and gives Max a look that answers his question.

Susie picks up the money and begins counting. Halfway through, she stops.

"You know, you might even have enough to pay for food while you're over there."

Dolly clasps her hands together.

"Have we done it?" she asks.

"Done what?"

Annie steps into the room in her pajamas. Runt is by her side.

"You're going to London!" Max exclaims. He snatches the money from the table and throws it into the air.

Annie is shocked and confused as the notes fall around her.

"What do you mean?"

"We raised enough money," says Bryan.

"But . . . how?"

"We all pitched in," says Dolly.

"Not just us," says Susie. "People in town. All your class-mates. Your teachers. They're all cheering you on, Annie. And you too, Runt."

Annie is at a loss for words. She looks up at Bryan with a tentative smile.

"Really? Is it true? It's not a Kind Lie? We can really go?"

"Really really," says Bryan.

Susie snaps back to business.

"Right. We'll have to sort out passports and flights and your accommodations. I'll have to map all your routes so you don't get lost. We'll have to arrange your registration with the Krumpet's Dog Show. Oh, there's so much to do!"

"I'd better put the practice course back together," Annie says to Runt.

Then she looks up at her family.

"Thank you, everyone," Annie begins, but she is inter-rupted by a knock at the door.

Everyone goes quiet. Bryan hurries down the hallway. He opens the door to reveal Earl Robert-Barren.

He wears a gray suit and a sour expression.

"Mr. Shearer, I have made repeated attempts to contact you today. I'm here to notify you that your sheep have yet again committed criminal trespass."

Bryan closes his eyes and shakes his head. "Earl, mate, I'm very sorry."

"I have conservatively estimated the cost of damages and loss of aquatic inventory to be twelve thousand dollars."

"*Twelve thousand dollars?* Where have you pulled that from?"

Everyone in the dining room is listening intently.

Earl is cold and curt and calculating.

"Furthermore, under clause four, subsection three of the Rural Ruminants Act within the Ovine Charter, I am entitled to take full possession of the offending herd as security until the agreed fee is paid in full. I am officially serving your legal notice. You have thirty days."

Earl hands Bryan a thick envelope.

Bryan tries to remain calm.

"Listen, Earl. There's no need for any of that. Me and Annie will come by first thing in the morning and round them up. The fence is almost fully repaired. I promise you this will be the last time it happens."

"Your proposal is denied. I withdraw all permissions for you to enter my property, Mr. Shearer, and be advised that doing so henceforth constitutes a criminal act."

Bryan's temper rises.

"A criminal act? There's only one criminal in Upson Downs, and that's *you*, mate. The only reason those sheep are pushing into your property is because you're holding our water hostage!"

Earl is unruffled and composed. "Mr. Shearer, defamatory accusations, at which I take considerable offense, will only contribute to your liability for damages."

"Well, here's a defamatory accusation for you, Earl: stuff your ransom. I'm fed up. I'm going to the police. I want my sheep back."

"Very well. Give Constable Bayleaf my earnest regards. I did speak with him only an hour ago, and he seemed very supportive of my actions. Mr. Shearer, I'm a reasonable man and I have given you reasonable terms. However, should you wish to challenge them, my advice is that you seek independent legal counsel."

"Like my father did? They squeezed us for our last dollar and did nothing with it."

"Alternatively," says Earl, looking around and licking his lips, "you can sell me your property. I've always admired it. There's no shame in admitting to your failures, Mr. Shearer. Some people just aren't suited to the farming life. Not every child can advance beyond their father's shadow."

Bryan slams the door so hard the walls shake.

When he turns around, his family is standing in the hallway, looking at him.

They drift back to the dining room.

After a moment of grim silence, Annie begins picking up the scattered notes. Then she hands all the money back to Susie.

THE MYSTERIOUS MUSTACHIOED MAN

The next day, Annie walks down the main street of Upson Downs with Runt by her side. She is on her way to the supermarket to spend her pocket money on Mush Canine Cuisine.

Suddenly, she stops. She takes three steps back.

There, in the window of Patel's Petals, is the rainbow rose.

Annie stares. It's strange and surprising to see it on display for everyone to admire. Then, like a curtain is being drawn back in her mind, she realizes that her father must have sacrificed it to get them to London.

Annie is proud that people in Upson Downs can see how beautiful the rose is, but she also feels a bit sad that he sold it, that it doesn't belong to him anymore.

Annie keeps walking but stops again, this time outside the real estate agency. The window is covered in photos of farms with banners that say: **For Sale! Urgent—Must Go! Bargain Price! Going Cheap! Under Offer! Sold! Sold! Sold! SOLD!**

Annie walks on. Her head is down, heavy with thoughts. She can't help worrying that their farm will be in the window next, and that Earl Robert-Barren might add it to his collection. She thinks of all the things she would have to leave behind. Her bedroom. Runt's doghouse. The shearing shed. The windmill and the Rainmaker. The secret greenhouse. The practice paddock. The dining room.

She wonders where they would go. She can't imagine living anywhere else.

Annie reminds herself of what Dolly told her, about being strong and never giving up. But it's hard not to feel hopeless, especially now that Earl Robert-Barren is holding their sheep hostage and demanding all that money.

There's only one thing to do, Annie decides. She *has* to get to London. And they *have* to win the Grand Championship at the Krumpet's Dog Show.

Suddenly, out of nowhere, a figure steps in front of her and blocks her path.

Annie stops. She looks up.

The man is short, and he wears a cream suit with a black shirt. He looks familiar, but Annie can't summon where she has seen him before. He wears thick glasses and a fedora hat. And most noticeably, his eyebrows and his mustache are incredibly thick and bushy.

"Good morning," the man says. "My name is Arthur Throwguls. I represent a syndicate of breeders who are very interested in acquiring talented canines."

He hands Annie a business card. It says:

> **ARTHUR THROWGULS**
> Talent Acquisition
> Pedigreedy Breeds
> **T:** 993-555-7823

"I'd like to congratulate you on your recent success at the National Titles. My clients are *very* impressed with your dog. In fact, they are willing to offer you one hundred and fifty thousand dollars for him."

Annie is taken aback.

"What do you mean? To *buy* Runt?"

"That is correct."

"To keep?"

"Yes."

"Forever?"

"Yes."

"But . . . he's my friend."

Arthur Throwguls leans down and speaks softly.

"Yes, but don't you want to save your farm, Annie? Don't you want your family to be happy? Isn't that more important?"

He straightens and reaches inside his jacket. He takes out a document and a pen.

"All you have to do is sign this transfer of ownership, and all your problems can be gone like *that!*"

Throwguls snaps his fingers theatrically.

The moment he does so, something very odd happens.

His left eyebrow drops to the ground.

"Your eyebrow just fell off," says Annie.

"No it didn't," says Arthur Throwguls, entirely aware that his eyebrow did indeed just fall off.

"It did. Look."

Annie points at it.

"That's not mine," Throwguls insists. He shakes his head in furious denial, which is enough to dislodge his *other* eyebrow, which also drops to the pavement. Runt sniffs it.

"Your other one just fell off."

"No it didn't."

"It really did," says Annie.

She picks them both up, holding them in her palm like two fuzzy caterpillars.

Arthur Throwguls begins to sweat. He glances around surreptitiously, as though he's wary of being seen. He feels his mustache start to peel away from his lip. He tries to speak quickly without moving his mouth.

"You would be wise to consider my offer, Annie Shearer. Think about all that money. One hundred and fifty *thousand* dollars. Don't you want to fix everything?"

And with that, he snatches his eyebrows from her, turns around, presses them back into place, and swiftly departs.

Annie looks down at Runt. Runt looks up at Annie.

Then Annie looks at the card again.

Her hand is trembling.

Later that afternoon, Annie knocks on the door of the secret greenhouse. Bryan opens it.

"You sold your special rose," says Annie.

"Yep."

Behind him, Annie can see empty spots on the shelves.

"You sold other plants too. So that we could go to London."

"And I'd do it again in a heartbeat," Bryan says.

"But that rose was really precious to you."

Bryan kneels down and looks Annie in the eyes.

"Not as precious as you are, mate. You, and your mum, your brother, Dolly—you'll always be most important to me. You'll always come first."

Annie gives it some thought.

"So . . . sometimes sacrificing something you love is the right thing to do?"

Bryan nods.

"Yeah, I s'pose it is."

HIGHBROW, LOWBROW

Fergus Fink reclines on a leather sofa in a room decorated with dozens of mirrors. He wears sandstone jodhpurs, a green blazer, and a plum silk cravat. On his chest lies a lazy black cat. Fergus strokes its fur and dotes on it.

"You're a magnificent creature, aren't you?"

The cat yawns and stretches, aware of its magnificence.

As Fergus takes a sip of brandy from a crystal goblet, there is a knock on the door.

"Enter!"

Arthur Throwguls steps into the room.

"Simpkins!" says Fergus, because, as you may have already guessed, Arthur Throwguls is Simpkins in a very poor disguise.

His fake bushy eyebrows sit absurdly high on his forehead.

"What on earth took you so long? Did she accept our offer?"

"Not quite, sir."

Fergus leaps to his feet. The black cat bolts from the room.

"Not *quite*? What do you mean? And why are you so surprised? You look like you've just seen a ghost."

Realizing, Simpkins hurriedly adjusts his eyebrows.

"It's just . . . well, she didn't answer one way or another. I did get the impression she was considering it carefully."

"How much did you offer?"

"One hundred and fifty thousand, like you ordered."

"And she didn't take it?"

"No, sir," says Simpkins, still fiddling with his eyebrows. He takes his hands away. They are now angled steeply inward, making him look very angry.

"Don't get cross with me!" says Fergus. "I'm not the one who failed to execute a perfectly simple assignment!"

"I'm sorry, sir," says Simpkins, dabbing his brows onto his forehead again.

"Well, did you raise the offer?"

"No, I didn't. I wasn't sure if I should. I mean, it's a lot of money."

Fergus throws his hands into the air, spilling some brandy.

"It's not as though I was ever going to actually *pay*, you mollusk! I just want that dog as far from London as possible!"

Tentatively, Simpkins removes his hands, but he's made a mess of his eyebrows again. One is high, the other low, giving him an air of disapproval.

"Oh, spare me your moral judgment, Simpkins! You knew the score. I want that runt out of the race, and you've failed me again!" Fergus waves him away. "You're dismissed. Go and run circuits with Chariot."

Simpkins nods. Then, on account of his allergy to cats, sneezes explosively. Simpkins checks his eyebrows, which are still intact. However, his mustache has flown from his lip and plopped into the goblet of brandy. He cringes, but Fergus hasn't noticed.

Fergus takes a sip and swishes the brandy in his mouth, relishing the taste.

"Well, go on, then. Get out of my sight."

Simpkins bows and leaves.

He walks quickly through the house, removing his silly hat and fake glasses and those bushy brows. He enters a dark, sparsely furnished room and flicks on the light. Chariot is locked inside a crate. Simpkins kneels and opens it, and Chariot bursts out, wagging her tail and licking him affectionately.

Simpkins smiles and rubs her fur.

"Yes, I know, I know," he says. "I love you too."

Simpkins stands. Chariot spins in circles, then leaps up into his arms.

"One day," Simpkins whispers, "you're going to come and live with me, and you'll never be locked up again."

THE IMPOSSIBLE CHOICE

That night, Annie sits on her bed, staring at the business card.

Runt is lying beside her, his snout resting on her knee.

It's an impossible choice.

With one phone call she can fix their problems. She can pay the overdraft on the overdraft. She can get their sheep back. She can save the farm.

But it will cost Annie her best and only friend. She will have to give Runt away. She can't imagine being without him.

Then she thinks about her dad sacrificing his rainbow rose, and how he knew it was the right thing to do. She thinks about how nice it is that everyone can see it now and appreciate its beauty.

She wonders if Runt would be happier at Pedigreedy Breeds. Maybe it would be somehow better there. Maybe they would be friendly, and he could eat Mush Canine Cuisine whenever he wanted.

Annie looks down at Runt. Runt looks up at Annie.

At the same time, in the dining room, Bryan is facing his own agonizing decision.

On the table in front of him is a big jar filled with the money they collected. On either side of it are his two options.

To the left is the official invitation to the Krumpet's Dog Show. To the right is the legal notice from Earl Robert-Barren. Bryan picks up the notice and reads it under his breath.

"*. . . failure to comply by the specified date will result in immediate seizure of property and assets . . .*"

Suddenly, the pages are snatched out of his hands.

"You're not paying that man a cent."

Bryan looks up. It's Dolly.

"He ruined your father," she says, sitting down. "I won't have him ruin you too."

"But we'll lose everything, Mum."

"Will we?"

"Yes. Read the document."

Dolly squints and looks it over.

"Doesn't say anything in here about losing me. Or Susie. Or the kids. Doesn't say anything about losing the memories we've made here. Or the love we have for each other."

"Well . . . *no*. But . . ."

"So we won't lose *everything*, will we?"

"No."

"It's not the roof that has value, Bryan, it's the people who live under it. That's worth more than money or land. And it's something that monster across the road will never, ever have. He'll never be able to buy it or seize it or collect it. Because it's *us*. It's *ours*."

Bryan blinks away tears.

Dolly rips up the legal notice into small pieces; then she pushes the invitation to the Krumpet's Dog Show in front of him.

"Go and see the world. Go and have an adventure with your daughter. You've worked so hard for so long, and you deserve it. This is the stuff that matters, this is the stuff you don't want to miss. And you don't know if you'll ever have this chance again. That girl and that dog are something special. And who knows? We might just win."

Back in her bedroom, Annie continues to stare at the card.

She still can't decide.

"The thing is," she says to Runt, "it's different from the rainbow rose, because you're not a plant. You're my family. It would be like selling Max or Grandma Dolly, and I could never do that. And you're not mine to sell, anyway. I don't own you. Nobody does. And nobody *should* either. You're here because you want to be. And I want to be here too. I really like our farm. It's my home. But I don't think I'd like it as much if you weren't here to share it with. It wouldn't be the same."

Annie rips up the card.

"And who knows?" she says. "We might just win."

TEAM SHEARER

The Shearers are running early.

Very early.

Once again, the family is crammed into their yellow sedan. But this time Susie is behind the wheel. She is as calm as a summer evening, weaving through the traffic with patience and poise.

"Are you sure you don't need directions?" Bryan asks.

"No thanks, dear. I've got it all mapped and memorized."

"How are we doing for time?" asks Dolly, peering anxiously out the window.

"Plenty to spare," says Susie.

Runt sits quietly and comfortably inside a traveling crate, squeezed between Annie and Dolly.

"Does anyone want this last sandwich?" Max asks, still chewing. "I think four's my limit."

"Save it for the trip home," says Susie, winking at Annie in the rearview mirror.

The Shearers stand by the check-in counter inside the airport terminal. Bryan, who has never been in a plane, looks nervous.

Susie gives them their final briefing.

"Okay, Annie, I've put both your passports inside *this* pocket of your tool belt. Don't lose them. Bryan, this satchel has all your documents and forms. I've also included some British pounds, directions to your accommodations, and a list of some interesting places to visit if you have the time. Got that?"

Annie and Bryan nod together.

Susie continues.

"Now, Bryan, don't recline your seat until you're up in the air. Also, don't introduce yourself to everyone on the plane. Annie, if you need help with anything, there will be a button at your seat. Press it and someone will come right over. Drink lots of water, and try to sleep as much as you can. It's a long flight. Yes?"

Annie and Bryan nod together.

Susie continues.

"It's going to be very cold over there, so I've knitted you both these matching beanies."

She hands them each a soft beanie made with multi-colored yarn. There are crimsons and golds and teal greens and royal blues and lavenders and apricots. Annie thinks they look a little like Bryan's rainbow rose.

"I used the wool from home, so you'll always have a bit of us with you. Make sure you wear them whenever you go out. They're nice and bright, so you won't lose each other in the crowds. Also, I've sewn in this tag with the address of your hotel, and I've hidden some money in them too, so if you do get lost, just wave down a black cab and show them your beanie."

"Is the queen's phone number in here as well?" Bryan asks.

Dolly fixes him with a look.

"Sorry," Bryan mutters. "They're brilliant, love."

"And here, Annie, look—I've knitted a jacket for Runt in the same colors."

"You've got a uniform," says Max. "Team Shearer!"

"Team Shearer," says Bryan. "I like that."

Annie takes the jacket.

"Thank you," she says.

An airline ground-crew clerk approaches them with a smile. He grabs the handle of Runt's traveling crate. "Okay, I can take your friend from here."

"Wait," says Annie.

She buries her face in Runt's rainbow jacket and nuzzles it. Then she invites her family to do the same.

The clerk, utterly confused by this bizarre ritual, watches with his eyebrows raised.

Then Annie kneels and opens the door of Runt's crate. She rolls the jacket into a tight log and puts it next to him.

"This way he can smell us all and he won't get too lonely," she explains. "You'll be okay, Runt, I promise. See you on the other side of the world."

The clerk picks up the crate.

"Look after that dog!" says Bryan.

"Right," says Susie. "I think that's everything. Oh, now, Runt's blinders are in your luggage. You've only got the one pair, so don't lose them, okay?"

Annie and Bryan nod together.

"Go give 'em a run for their money," says Dolly.

They exchange hugs. Bryan gives Susie a tight squeeze.

"Thanks, love," he whispers. "For everything."

Annie and Bryan pull on their matching beanies. They bump knuckles.

"Righto, Team Shearer," says Bryan. "Let's go win this thing."

Bryan twists around anxiously in his seat as the plane prepares for takeoff. He makes a note of the emergency exits, then carefully examines a laminated card that describes what to do if the plane is plummeting to the ground.

"Strange to think that we're about to be floating in the sky in a big metal tube for the next few hours, isn't it?"

"I suppose so," says Annie, who isn't frightened at all. "A

few hours isn't that much, though. There's a bird that can stay in the air for ten whole months without landing once. It's called a common swift."

"Really?"

"Really really."

"But where do they sleep?"

"In the sky."

"While they're flying?"

"Yes."

"Well, I take my hat off to them for that. Or my beanie, I should say. If *I* get any sleep on this thing, it'll be a miracle. What are they called again?"

"The common swift."

"Got a bit ripped off with their name, didn't they? Common swift? Should be . . . the *tireless flapper.* Or what about this: the *golden glider.* Where do they name birds, anyway? Maybe we should have a word with them."

"They classify animals at the Natural History Museum. Plants too. It's in London. I'd like to go there very much. Charles Darwin used to work there."

"Oh yeah? Let's whack it on the itinerary."

"It's already on there."

"It is? She's pretty amazing, your mum."

Bryan is interrupted by a flight attendant. He flinches, still on edge.

"Here you are."

The attendant hands him a small packet of snacks.

"Oh, yeah, righto," says Bryan, digging into his back pocket for his wallet. "What's the damage on those?"

"They're complimentary, sir," says the attendant, who looks at him as though he might have actually been born yesterday.

Bryan turns to Annie with wide eyes.

"Free snacks!"

Annie smiles.

Not long after, the plane starts to move. Bryan grips his armrest as though he's been struck by lightning. Annie puts her hand over his.

"Dad, we will be okay."

A few hours later, Bryan is snoring. Drool pours from the side of his mouth as he sleeps in the sky more soundly than a common swift, or, indeed, a *golden glider*.

Beside him, Annie is wide-awake, watching old clips from the Krumpet's Dog Show that she has saved on her laptop.

The lady in the seat beside her notices and leans across.

"I see you're a fan of Krumpet's," she says.

"Not really," says Annie, eyes glued to the screen. "But me and Runt are going to win it, and then we're going to pay the overdraft on the overdraft."

The woman nods slowly and gives Annie a peculiar look.

LONDON

Weary and bleary, Team Shearer takes the train from Heathrow Airport into the city of London.

Annie is transfixed by the unfamiliar world that passes by the window. The sky is gray and the buildings are brown, with flashes of green lawns.

"All the houses are so scrunched up together," she says.

Bryan doesn't respond. He is busy reading Susie's instructions.

Annie tugs his sleeve and points. And Bryan looks out at a new country for the first time.

"Wow," he says with wonder. "Look at all that."

The train stops at Paddington Station.

They step onto the platform and stare up at the high curved ceiling before they're quickly nudged and brushed by passengers coming and going. They wheel their luggage out into the street.

"So," says Bryan, "we can take a long walk and potentially get lost, or be sensible and take a taxi."

"Let's walk," says Annie.

It's cold outside. Annie is thankful for her beanie. She releases Runt from his crate, fits him into his jacket, and lets him stretch his legs. He lifts his snout and sniffs the air, trying to make sense of where he is.

The streets are busy. People walk quickly. Everyone seems to be in a hurry. Runt presses his body against Annie's leg.

They walk for a long time, past old buildings, past new buildings, past pubs and restaurants, past shops and offices and apartments.

Eventually they stop at the entrance to a dark alleyway littered with bins and boxes.

"I think it's down here," says Bryan.

Annie peers down the lane, uncertain. "Are you sure?"

"Definitely sure," says Bryan, who is not sure at all.

He checks the map with Susie's directions for a third time. A small drop of water spatters onto the page. Then another.

It starts to rain.

Annie and Runt shelter in the doorway of a closed barbershop. But Bryan stays out in the open. He folds the map and tucks it under his arm. He removes his beanie, tilts his head back, closes his eyes, and feels rain on his face for the first time in more than four hundred days. He takes a deep breath.

Annie is tempted to call out, but her dad looks so calm and content. The shower passes quickly, and Bryan opens his eyes as though he's just woken from a lovely dream. He shakes his head like a wet dog.

"That felt good," he says. "Come on, let's check out our digs."

After four flights of stairs, Bryan and Annie stagger into their very small, very shabby hotel room.

The wallpaper is the color of mustard and peels at the corners. The carpet is blue and has dark stains. The room smells musty, as though the air is older than Bryan. Somewhere, a tap is dripping. There are two small beds, with folded towels at the ends. Bryan picks one up and dries the rain from his face and hair.

Then his phone rings. It's Susie.

Bryan answers.

"Yes, love, we've just stepped in now. . . . No, we didn't get lost. . . . How's the room? Well . . ."

Bryan pauses and looks around. He winks at Annie.

"You didn't tell me we were staying at Buckingham Palace! It's amazing, love. Absolutely deluxe. Very spacious. Full of . . . character. It's very clean."

Bryan wipes a layer of grime from the doorframe with his finger.

"How's the view? Hang on, let me have a look. . . ."

Bryan pulls back the gray curtains to reveal a brick wall. He bites his knuckle to stop himself from laughing.

"Oh, Susie, the view is gorgeous. Yeah, really. Goes for *miles.* I think I can see London Bridge from here."

Annie smiles.

"Yes. . . . Yes. . . . Yes, okay, I will do."

Bryan hangs up.

"Your mum says she loves you and to make sure you brush your teeth and your hair before you go to sleep."

Annie heaves her suitcase onto the closest bed and opens it. Along with her clothes, she has packed Dolly's boxing gloves, half a dozen tins of Mush Canine Cuisine, and Runt's food bowl.

Runt wags his tail in anticipation as Annie prepares his favorite meal.

She cracks the can. The meat wobbles and plops. And Runt dives in, nudging the bowl around the room.

"Look at him go," says Bryan. "Gee, he loves that stuff, doesn't he?"

Annie sits on the bed and reads through the Krumpet's Dog Show schedule.

"We should try to get there early," she says. "The qualifying heats are in the morning, and the final is at night, if we make it that far."

"Of course you'll make the final."

"You don't know that."

"I do. You're the best of the bunch, you two."

"Is that another one of your Kind Lies?" Annie asks.

"I don't know what you're talking about," says Bryan, who knows exactly what she's talking about.

"So you can really see London Bridge from our window?"

"Sure you can," says Bryan. "If you knock a few buildings over."

Annie rolls her eyes.

"Well, we had better get some rest, then," says Bryan. "Big day tomorrow."

He eases himself onto his bed and lies down. Slowly, the mattress sinks so low that he almost disappears, as though he's in a deep hammock.

"I think I'm stuck again."

THE TALE OF GORGEOUS GEORGE

In 1897, there lived a man by the name of Kingsley Krumpet.

Kingsley was a confectionery salesman, and he spent his days roaming the streets of London selling sweets from a wooden cart.

Wearing a straw boater hat and a red-and-white-striped jacket, Kingsley Krumpet would ring a handbell and shout through a brass megaphone: "Krumpet's Confectionery, passin' through! Raspberry drops! Peppermint suckers! Humbugs! Fizzy lemon delights! Toffee! Licorice! Sugared almonds! Caramel clinkers! Six for a penny! Mystery bags for thruppence! Krumpet's Confectionery, at your service!"

The cart was pulled by Kingsley's reliable companion, a border collie called Gorgeous George.

As his name suggested, Gorgeous George was a very

handsome dog. People stopped in the street to remark on his shiny coat, his excellent posture, and his healthy size. Gorgeous George had blue eyes and a black diamond-shaped patch on his white chest. He also had a very friendly disposition. Children rushed to pat Gorgeous George, and he licked their sticky fingers while they sucked on their sweets.

Nobody loved Gorgeous George more than Kingsley Krumpet. Every night he washed and brushed the dog's fur and fed him fresh bones and offcuts from the local butcher.

Then, one awful morning, Kingsley Krumpet woke up and discovered his front door was open, a vase had been smashed, and Gorgeous George was gone.

His faithful friend had been stolen.

Despairing, Kingsley searched everywhere, ringing his handbell and calling for Gorgeous George. He reported the dognapping to the police and pasted notices on every wall for thirty miles, but Gorgeous George could not be found.

Kingsley's desperation mounted. He was almost out of ideas. But then, in a stroke of genius, Kingsley Krumpet hatched a very clever plan.

He began advertising a Finest Dog Competition, offering a twenty-pound prize for the best-looking canine in London. To his way of thinking, the scoundrel who took Gorgeous George wouldn't be able to resist the opportunity to enter such an attractive creature, and Kingsley would be reunited with his dear friend.

To make his ruse more believable, Kingsley chose six

breeds to feature: spaniels, poodles, bloodhounds, corgis, terriers, and, of course, border collies. He offered an award for each category, and one grand prize for the overall Best in Show.

Kingsley left flyers in places where dog-thieving rascals might gather: pubs of low reputation, gambling dens, race-tracks, and the most dangerous parts of town.

But word spread farther and faster than he could have imagined.

Kingsley had hoped a few dozen people and their dogs might turn up to Hazelbrush Green on that sunny Saturday, but to his surprise and horror and delight, hundreds descended upon the park to watch and participate in Kingsley Krumpet's Finest Dog Competition.

The event was chaotic. Leashes were tangled. Dogs chased other dogs. Dogs chased ducks around the lake. Dogs chased squirrels up trees. Dogs chased children and pigeons and dragonflies.

Eventually, Kingsley managed to sort everyone into their breeds, and the show commenced. The audience cheered and laughed as entrants were paraded in a circle, and Kingsley pretended to judge them carefully. However, he only really paid close attention to the border collies. He made them walk past three times while he searched for Gorgeous George. But, with a deep sigh, he conceded that his friend was not among them, and his clever plan had not worked.

Still, Kingsley Krumpet stayed true to his word. He gave

special ribbons to the winners of each category, and awarded the grand prize to a Pembroke Welsh corgi called Nubbins.

The crowds had a marvelous time. Many congratulated Kingsley Krumpet for hosting such an enjoyable day and vowed to return next year. Even Kingsley had to admit that, despite his disappointment, it had been a jolly affair. But once everyone had departed, he was again all alone, and many pounds poorer.

Kingsley Krumpet's Finest Dog Competition had been accidentally so successful that he made all the newspapers. In every interview, he appealed to the public to come forward if they encountered a handsome border collie with sparkling blue eyes and a black diamond patch on his chest.

But nobody ever did.

Without Gorgeous George to pull his cart, Kingsley stopped selling his sweets. Before long, he was out of money and full of sorrow. He lost his home and sold his belongings, and he was soon living beneath a bridge beside Borough Market. The only possessions he couldn't bear to part with were his red-and-white-striped jacket and his straw boater, both of which were tattered and filthy.

Then came a miracle.

One day, while scrounging in an alley for scraps, Kingsley happened upon a skinny black dog with matted hair who was doing the same. The dog looked up. He had very blue eyes. And though the dog was very dirty, Kingsley could see a faint diamond patch over his heart.

It was Gorgeous George. His friend recognized him immediately and leaped into his arms. The two were together again.

With Gorgeous George back, so too returned Kingsley Krumpet's spirit. He washed his jacket and repaired his hat, and he began spreading the word about the *second* annual Krumpet's Finest Dog Show.

The rules were the same as the year before, with one exception: it cost a single shilling to enter.

The big day arrived. This time, more than a thousand attended, bringing their pets and picnic lunches and flasks of tea. The dogs put on a brilliant show. Ribbons and prizes were awarded, but the biggest winner was Kingsley Krumpet, because he had made a small fortune.

The Krumpet's Finest Dog Show got bigger and grander every year. Soon it moved to a football stadium to accommodate the crowds. Kennel clubs and pedigree breeders sponsored the competition, which gave it international prestige. Kingsley expanded the categories and added other disciplines, including what would become the most exciting and popular event of all: the Agility Course Grand Championship.

The success of the dog show brought Kingsley Krumpet great wealth, but he never forgot his time of bleak misfortune living alone beneath the bridge. He gave most of his money away to dog shelters and soup kitchens and families who had lost their homes.

On weekends he would wear the same striped jacket

and the same straw boater, and he would harness Gorgeous George to a new wooden cart. Together they visited the poorest parts of the city, giving away sweets to hungry children.

Kingsley Krumpet never discovered who had stolen his loyal friend. However, one Sunday, they passed a milkman who spilled a crate of empty bottles. The glass smashed against the cobbles, spooking Gorgeous George, who bolted away with the cart clattering behind him. He was found cowering behind a blackberry bush half a mile away.

As Kingsley soothed him, he remembered the broken vase from that fateful morning. Perhaps Gorgeous George had bumped the table, smashed the vase, and simply fled in fear, somehow opening the front door with his scrambling. To be safe, Kingsley removed all breakable items from his home and kept his doors forever locked.

In the summer of 1908, King Edward VII was a guest of the Krumpet's Dog Show. He even entered his own beloved pet, a wire fox terrier called Caesar, who was awarded Best in Show. The following year, King Edward repaid the gesture by knighting Kingsley Krumpet at Buckingham Palace. King Edward joked that Caesar still had the highest honor. The king became a patron of the competition and decreed that the Krumpet's Dog Show was a British institution, granting it an official royal title.

Upon the death of Sir Kingsley Krumpet in 1963, a bronze statue was built to commemorate his remarkable life, with one of Gorgeous George sitting ever faithful by his side. Sir Kingsley Krumpet, of course, was immortalized in his striped jacket and straw boater.

It became a common superstition for people to rub the diamond patch of Gorgeous George, because doing so would bring them luck and love. Over time, so many hands have touched the dog's chest that the outer layer has worn away and his heart glows golden.

Their statues remain to this day outside the Royal Canine Exhibition Center. And beneath them, right now, stands Annie Shearer and her best friend, Runt, all the way from Upson Downs.

Annie stands on her tiptoes and reaches out, placing her palm against the heart of Gorgeous George. And despite the crisp, cold London air, it feels warm to the touch.

THE BIG DAY BEGINS

The lobby of the Royal Canine Exhibition Center is teeming with people.

There are banners advertising Mush Canine Cuisine and other dog foods. There are stalls selling grooming accessories and shampoos. There are vets talking about flea collars and deworming medication. There are kennels offering obedience boot camps for naughty puppies. There are displays of chew toys, throw toys, comfort toys, and training toys.

Annie and Runt are both overwhelmed. They stand beside a huge cardboard cutout of a Saint Bernard, waiting for Bryan to return from the registration booth.

Finally, Annie spots a colorful beanie bobbing among the crowd.

"Over here!" Annie waves.

Bryan sees them and works his way over, puffing his cheeks and carrying a large envelope.

"Worse than a mob of sheep, this lot."

He drapes a lanyard around Annie's neck.

"That's your pass. Don't lose it. Okay, hold my hand, stick close, we're going in. You two ready?"

Annie looks down at Runt. Runt looks up at Annie.

Annie nods.

The backstage area of the Krumpet's Dog Show is an enormous room filled with show dogs and their owners, who, it must be said, look remarkably alike.

It's a hive of activity. Poodles are primped on trestle tables. Pomeranians are blow-dried. Spitzes are spritzed. Afghan hounds are combed. All manner of fur is brushed and fluffed and snipped and straightened.

Team Shearer slowly heads toward the agility course section.

Bryan sees a Great Dane being thoroughly massaged. "Can I be next? Had a long flight over. Bit tight in the lower lumbar."

The masseur pauses to give him a humorless, irritated look.

Bryan widens his eyes at Annie, and they walk away quickly. However, they don't make it far, as they soon encounter a familiar face.

"Well, well, well. I see you've scrounged up enough coins to make the trip across," says Fergus Fink. Simpkins and Chariot stand behind him. "Waste of money, if you ask me."

Fergus is dressed head to toe in white. He wears a cable-knit sweater with his initials embroidered in gold thread, as though he's about to step onto center court for the 1923 Wimbledon final.

Below, Runt and Chariot sniff each other cautiously.

At the same time, a lost little pug wearing a blue bow waddles over and inspects Fergus's left ankle as he continues speaking.

"You may have been notified that a formal complaint was submitted to the Krumpet's Dog Show Fairness and Ethics Committee regarding your continued abuse of the rules and regulations, but it seems they are intent on staining the integrity of this hallowed event by permitting you to compete."

Bryan and Annie observe the pug lifting his leg and using Fergus's ankle as a bathroom.

"Integrity is important, isn't it?" says Bryan, trying to keep a straight face.

"Without it, we have nothing," Fergus declares dramatically.

"Well, I'm sorry to say the integrity of your trousers has been stained, mate."

Fergus glances down and recoils in disgust. The pug scarpers, leaving behind a warm puddle and a very annoyed man.

"Simpkins! Fetch a towel! I've been defiled."

Annie opens a pocket of her tool belt and takes out some tissues. She offers them to Fergus.

Fergus narrows his eyes and scowls.

"Enjoy your morning. I doubt I'll be seeing you tonight."

He storms off, his wet left shoe squelching.

Before he follows, Simpkins bows and offers a kind, tentative smile.

"Good luck out there," he whispers, and it sounds as though he means it.

BASIL AND CAMILLA

Since it was first broadcast in 1971, the same two commentators have presented the Krumpet's Dog Show to more than a hundred countries worldwide. Their names are Basil Peppercorn and Camilla Crowne-Jewel. You may have heard of them.

Today, Basil wears a tweed coat and a tartan tie, and Camilla wears a silk blouse beneath a lavender jacket. They sit behind a desk in a studio inside the Royal Canine Exhibition Center, with the arena floor in full view behind them. They both straighten their posture and look at the camera as the program returns from a commercial break.

Camilla smiles. Her voice is soft and prim and proper.

"Welcome back to the Krumpet's Dog Show. We're deep in the qualifying heats of the Agility Course Grand Championship, and it has been a marvelous display so far."

Basil's voice is rich and deep and posh.

"Quite right, Camilla. It's rather first-rate and splendid to watch."

Camilla nods. "Now, the top *five* dogs from each of the *two* qualifying pools will earn the right to compete in the final this evening. Presently in the lead in this pool is Hänsel, a German shepherd from Salzburg. Close behind is Moki, a shiba inu from Osaka Prefecture, who gave an utterly clinical performance."

"Quite right, Camilla."

"And in third place we have Moose, a Saskatoonian husky, who, you may recall, famously won this event five years ago. He's still formidable, but there comes a time when we all must accept that our best days are behind us, Basil."

"Are you referring to me or the husky?"

"I think I'll leave that for our viewers to decide."

"Quite right, Camilla."

"Fourth in the current pool standings is a veteran competitor from Australia, Fergus Fink, with his whippet, Chariot."

"Fink has an enviable heritage himself," says Basil. "Five generations of Finks have won here at the Krumpet's Dog Show. An extraordinary dynasty. Though, it must be said, as competitive as he has proven to be, Fergus Fink has yet to win a major event either Down Under or up over."

"I would imagine the pressure to break through and succeed weighs heavier with each passing year, Basil."

"Quite right, Camilla. In fact, one wonders if it could provide the motive for desperate acts of villainy."

"Perhaps so. Particularly if there were a compelling new contender from his home country."

"Which, of course, there is. And what a remarkable story. Annie Shearer, from the quiet little town of Upson Downs, is the youngest handler in the history of this event, at just eleven years of age."

"Extraordinary, Basil. But even more fascinating is her dog, Runt, who is an adopted stray, and whose breed and lineage is a fabulous mystery."

"Quite right, Camilla. And if that weren't enough, in a somewhat controversial turn of events, Runt will also be competing in blinders. Another first for the Krumpet's Dog Show."

"I suppose not everybody loves an audience."

"Certainly not an issue for you over the years, Camilla."

"Indeed. Well, they're the talk of the tournament and an outside chance to win, having claimed the Australian National Title. We're willing Annie and Runt to make the final this evening, and the good news is they're up next. We hope you'll stay tuned."

"Quite right," says Basil. "Quite right."

QUALIFICATIONS

A dim access corridor connects the backstage area to the arena floor.

Annie is called forward by a volunteer, a young woman with a ponytail who is dressed all in black and speaks softly into a headset.

"Okay, Annie. They're ready for you. Are you all set?"

"One second," says Annie.

She takes Runt's blinders from her tool belt. Then she kneels and fits them securely. Satisfied, she looks up and nods.

"Great, just follow me through," says the volunteer, who then turns to Bryan. "I'm afraid you'll have to wait here, sir. Competitors only."

Bryan is so nervous and overawed that he is unable to speak. He nods and pumps his fist once.

The volunteer opens a small gate, and Annie and Runt step through and follow her.

At the end of the access corridor, the Krumpet's Dog Show arena reveals itself. The lights are bright. The crowd sits high and steep. The floor matting is green and pristine. The obstacles are neatly arranged. It is a world away from Annie's practice paddock.

Television cameras point from each corner. There are officials and timekeepers and event staff who look busy and professional. The referee stands ready. On the far side of the arena is the Agility Course Grand Championship Cup. It's silver, shiny, and bigger than Annie.

An announcement blares across the arena.

"Please welcome, all the way from Upson Downs, Australia, our youngest ever handler, Annie Shearer with Runt!"

The crowd applauds. The volunteer smiles and gestures for Annie to enter the arena floor. Annie steps out with Runt alongside her. She has watched so many clips of past events that everything looks strangely familiar.

As soon as the audience sees her, their cheering grows louder. Annie and Runt are an instant crowd favorite. Annie is grateful for their support, but she wishes the arena was empty.

The referee points Annie toward the starting line.

"Thank you," says Annie, but the crowd is so loud she can't be heard.

She looks up. Above her is an enormous video screen showing a live feed. Annie watches herself walking, her brown hair poking out from under her rainbow beanie, her tool belt flapping against her thighs. She looks *big*. It makes her think of Grandma Dolly. Her hands ball into fists, and she feels determined.

She sits Runt behind the starting line, and she squats down to speak to him.

"I'm right here, Runt. Same as always. It's just me and you. There's lots of noise, but we're the only ones here. Keep your eyes on me, and do your best. It's just like we're at home."

Runt's head is low. He sniffs the starting line tentatively.

Annie backs away from him slowly, making sure she stays in his narrow field of view. She's worried about him. Runt looks uncomfortable and distracted. She's tempted to walk back and reassure him again, but the referee hurries her up.

"Take your position!" he calls out.

The crowd hushes.

Annie holds her breath.

Her magic finger is pointed at the ceiling.

She waits for the chimes.

Three . . . two . . . one . . .

"*Go, go, go!* Come on, Runt! Let's go! Go!"

There's a tiny hint of hesitation, but to Annie's relief, Runt reacts. After a slow start, he sprints and soars over the first hurdle. In the back of her mind, though, Annie knows that they're already behind.

"Get around, get around! Through here! That's it, Runt! That's it!"

Runt turns sharply and enters the tunnel, flying out the end and zipping between the slalom poles.

"Weave! Weave! Weave! Now get around! Hup! Hup! That's it! Hold! Hold! Wait. . . . Let's go!"

Runt darts up the seesaw, teeters, then bolts down the slope, around to the long jump, and back through the second tunnel, dips beneath the low beam, vaults another high hurdle, gets up and over the balance beam with ease, and flies through the hoop jump.

The crowd is loud and delighted, willing him on.

"Get around, get around, *run, run, run!*"

Annie pushes him hard, trying to make up the lost time. She guides him into a sharp turn, and Runt responds so quickly that his back legs slip from under him on the smooth carpeting. The crowd gasps as he skitters.

On the sidelines, Bryan winces and goes weak at the knees.

But Runt recovers and makes a desperate dash for the finishing line. He is a brown blur across the length of the arena.

The crowd roars.

Annie catches up with Runt. She is out of breath, but Runt is barely panting.

The referee shows a green paddle. No penalties.

The crowd looks to the scoreboard. So does Bryan.

Annie is afraid to look up. She knows it's not their best time, but it might be enough.

Her heart is thumping.

She lifts her head.

38.03.

Fifth place. Just below Fergus Fink.

The stadium announcer confirms it.

"It's a qualifying time, folks! Annie Shearer and Runt are through to the final! Give her a hand."

Bryan spreads his hands in the air and dances giddily on the spot.

Annie, however, doesn't match his enthusiasm as she walks off the arena floor.

Neither does Fergus Fink, who watches on a wall-mounted television in the backstage area. He scowls. Then he turns to Simpkins, seething.

"Simpkins," he says. "Get the briefcase."

Bryan holds up his palm to invite a victorious high five as Annie returns to the backstage area.

"You did it! You're through!"

Annie leaves him hanging. Her head is down. She seems disappointed.

Bryan is worried.

"Is everything all right, mate? What's the matter?"

Annie shrugs.

"We only came in fifth."

"*Only?* Love, you two were the fifth fastest in the *world.*"

"But fifth isn't enough," says Annie. "Fifth doesn't fix anything. And all those people at home who helped us get here—I'm going to let them down too."

Bryan takes a big deep breath.

Around them, busy volunteers walk past carrying the dismantled obstacles from the course, as the arena floor is quickly cleared to make room for the show dogs. They place the equipment in a roped-off section with a small sign that reads: **Do Not Enter.**

Bryan looks at all the handlers fussing anxiously over their show dogs. They groom and they spray, they fluff and they comb, they clip nails and they brush teeth, they practice routines and obedience drills. The tension is contagious. Nobody is smiling or enjoying themselves.

"Come on," he says. "We've got a few hours up our sleeve. Let's go do something *fun.*"

KEY TO THE CITY

It's a gray, gloomy afternoon as Team Shearer strolls through London.

They find themselves in Piccadilly Circus, with its grand old buildings and brash electronic screens. The loud crowds and black cabs and red buses make Runt nervous, so they veer into quieter streets for a while.

As they amble down a cobbled lane, Bryan stops abruptly.

He stares at a storefront with flaking blue paint. Above the window in big brass letters, it says:

HUMBLE PIES & MASH

"Humble Pie!" Annie says.

"It's just like home."

"Look!" Annie points at a blackboard beside the entrance. In chalk are the words **Best Jellied Eels in London**.

"Jellied *eels*?" Bryan exclaims. "Not even your mum has thought of that."

He raises his eyebrows, tempted.

"You hungry?" he asks.

Inside, they sit at a small table. Runt lies at Annie's feet.

A man with a shaved head and faded tattoos steps out from behind the kitchen counter. He slides a plate and a bowl in front of Bryan, then wipes his hands on a filthy apron.

"There y'are, guv'nor."

Annie and Bryan stare at the plate. There's a flat pie surrounded by pillows of mashed potatoes and covered in what appears to be green slime. Sure enough, the accompanying bowl contains little white crescent moons suspended in a clear jelly.

"Are those bits of eel?" Annie asks.

The man winks.

"Put 'air on your chest, they will. Need anyfin' else, give me a shout."

With trepidation, Bryan plucks a nugget of eel from the goo and sets about building a forkful of pie and mash and slime. He exhales to prepare himself, then shovels it all into his mouth. He chews twice and freezes.

He stares at Annie.

Annie's lips twitch. She tries not to smile.

"Is it that bad?" she whispers.

Bryan shakes his head and swallows.

"Annie, it's *delicious*," he says.

"You don't have to tell a Kind Lie—he can't hear you."

"I'm serious! Try some."

Annie takes a bite.

"It's actually really good," she agrees. "I like the slime."

Bryan takes another bite and nods, his mouth full.

"Dondell yermahder."

"What?"

Bryan swallows and tries again.

"Don't tell your mother."

With the Humble Pie demolished in a short time, Team Shearer continues their journey.

They soon find themselves in a lush park. Pigeons nod as they hustle along the path. Annie spots a squirrel zipping up the trunk of a tree. And despite the blanket of clouds overhead, she is surprised to see a large man with a mustache sunbaking on the grass, lying shirtless on his back like a pink walrus on a green iceberg, and probably just as cold.

Then the park opens up, and appearing before them is a magnificent building. Bryan and Annie and Runt follow the high spikes of its boundary fence to an enormous black iron gate bearing two golden crests. They peer through it. Outside the entrance are guards in red jackets and big furry hats.

"I'll be stuffed," says Bryan. "It's Buckingham Palace."

"Do you think the queen's in there right now?" asks Annie.

"Pretty sure she is."

Annie is awestruck by the size of it.

"Do you think she has just one bedroom that she uses, or lots?"

Bryan thinks about it.

"Good question. I'd say she sleeps in a different room every night to keep the maids on their toes. But she only uses one toilet, which she calls the Throne Room."

Annie smiles and rolls her eyes.

Bryan tests the iron bars and is impressed.

"Got to get a set of these for the farm."

But Annie isn't listening. She's thinking about all those empty rooms. She wonders if the queen ever gets lonely.

Annie turns and spots a souvenir stand nearby. It gives her an idea.

She walks over with Runt and takes a coin and a pencil from her tool belt. She buys a postcard featuring Buckingham Palace on a sunny day, then sits on a nearby bench and begins writing.

> Dear Bernadette Box,
>
> We are at Buckingham Palace, and I thought about you because the queen also has a big front gate to keep people out. It looks a bit scary from the outside, but I'm sure she's really nice, just like you.
>
> I didn't get a chance to say thank you for helping us.

Maybe one day you can come to visit us in
Upson Downs. You should meet my grandma
Dolly. I think you would really like her.

Your friend,
Annie

P.S. We made the final.

Later, they walk along a path by a narrow canal. The water is dark and murky and carpeted with sludgy patches of duckweed. Annie admires the colorful houseboats moored in a long line.

They pass under a bridge, and on the other side they see an old man who appears to be fishing by hand with a thick line. He reels it in slowly. He wears leather gloves, gum boots, and a flat cap.

"Any bites?" Bryan asks.

The man laughs, and they soon see why.

At the end of the rope is a powerful magnet, the size and shape of a tin of cat food. Runt sniffs at it, then rears back. The man explains that he is fishing for treasure.

"Treasure? What sorts of things do you find?" Annie asks.

"What *don't* I find is more to the point. Cutlery. Lots of old computers and phones, these days. Coins. Nuts and bolts and fixtures. Door hinges and handles. Toasters. Bicycles. Scooters. Railway spikes. Batteries. Engine parts. Shopping trolleys. Pots. Pans. Pipes. Scissors. You name it. Figure I'm doing my bit to clean up."

The man tosses the magnet back into the water and slowly drags the rope in.

"Some very interesting finds, of course," he says. "Guns. Knives. Shrapnel bombs from the war. Couple of grenades too. Always a bit concerning, live ammunition. Have to call the police in, and they shut the canal down and evacuate the area. It's a whole circus."

He pulls up the magnet and inspects his haul. A drill bit, a whisk from an electric eggbeater, and a whistle. He plucks them off the magnet and drops them into a big bucket.

"What's the most valuable thing you've ever found?" Annie asks.

"Ooh, I'll never tell," the man says, and winks. "You want a go?"

Annie nods. "Okay."

"Pop these gloves on. Here you are. Now give it a bit of a swing, like a pendulum. Then let her go."

Annie tosses in the magnet. It kerplunks on the far side of the canal.

"Now just drag it in and see what sticks."

Slowly, Annie pulls the rope in.

The man crouches down.

"You really want to know the most valuable thing I've found out here?" he asks.

"Yes, please."

"The meaning of life," the man says.

Annie is confused.

"What do you mean?"

"See, every time I toss the line out, there's a chance I'll attract something good. Nothing beats that thrill, that little bit of hope. It's good for the soul, innit? Keeps you lively, keeps you guessing. Don't get disappointed if you come up short. Just keep trying, keep hoping. Take it from an old man—that's what we're all here to do. To keep trying and hoping and waiting for something good to come our way. That's the meaning of life."

Annie thinks about it and nods.

She fishes the magnet out of the water. There's something small stuck to the bottom. She picks it off and inspects it.

It's an old key.

"There you are!" says the man. "That's a good find, that."

He gives it a brisk scratch with a wire brush and wipes it down with a rag. It's about five inches long and looks as though it could be a hundred years old.

"It's all yours," says the man, presenting it to her.

"Are you sure?" Annie asks. "What if there's a treasure chest in there that it opens?"

"Then I'll have to use one of those grenades, won't I? You keep it. I insist. A little key from the waters of England. May it open many doors for you. Good luck."

"Thank you," says Annie as she tucks the key into her tool belt. "You're very nice."

SABOTAGE

At the same moment, a few miles away, deep inside the Royal Canine Exhibition Center, there stands a man who is *not* very nice and who never attracts good things.

That man, as you may have guessed, is Fergus Fink.

In view of the restricted area where the agility course obstacles are stored, Simpkins places a black briefcase onto a small table. The side of the case displays the same monogram as his outfit: *FF.*

Fergus Fink glances over each shoulder, making sure the coast is clear. Then he unclasps the briefcase and cracks it open.

Inside there are three small glass spray bottles nested in a foam tray. Each bottle features a different label. One has a picture of a bone. Another has a picture of a cat. The last has a picture of a sock.

Fergus points to each as he quickly explains to Simpkins.

"Listen carefully. This here is Distilled Essence of Treat. Spritz it on the slalom poles, right at the base. This bottle is Eau de Feline. Spray it around the entrance and the exit of the tunnels. And this one is Pungent Perfume of Old Socks. Spread it around the hoop jump and the seesaw. Use each sparingly. These scents are *extremely concentrated*. A little will go a very long way. Got that? Now. Move quickly and quietly, and make sure Chariot has her nose blocked before the final. And remember, if anyone sees you, tell them you're an Official Equipment Inspector. If that doesn't work, *run*. If you're apprehended, deny everything."

Simpkins nods, but his legs are frozen by hesitation. He can't move them.

"What are you doing?" Fergus whispers. "Go on!"

Simpkins looks pained.

Then he reaches out and shuts the briefcase.

"I can't do it," he says.

"Yes you can. There is nobody around. It's now or never! Go!" Fergus insists.

"No," says Simpkins. "I mean . . . I *won't* do it. It's cheating."

Fergus is dumbfounded. "Of *course* it's cheating! What's *wrong* with you?"

"I'm very sorry," says Simpkins, directing his apology to Chariot, who sits in her crate and pokes her nose through the grille.

Simpkins sighs, turns, and starts to walk away.

Fergus is momentarily stunned, then quickly furious. Red-faced, he stomps his foot.

"*Simpkins!* Get *back* here! Or you will be *fired*!"

But Simpkins no longer obeys. He disappears down a corridor, heart pounding.

Fuming, Fergus opens the briefcase and collects the bottles.

"Fine," he says. "I shall do it myself."

THE WORLD IS WATCHING

"Wake up! Wake up!"

Half a world away in Upson Downs, it's the middle of the night. Susie knocks on Max's bedroom door, then steps inside to rouse him. To her surprise, he is already awake. Max is sitting up in bed, typing and scrolling on his laptop with his one good hand.

"You've been pecking at that keyboard like an old hen for days. What are you up to?" Susie asks.

"Nothing," says Max.

"Well, it doesn't seem like nothing. Come on! It's almost time!"

"I'll be out in a bit. I'm nearly finished."

Susie narrows her eyes. "You had better not be planning another stunt," she says.

"Shh!" says Max. "I'm concentrating."

Susie lingers for a moment, then leaves.

When Max steps into the lounge room, still carrying his laptop, Dolly and Susie are on the couch in front of the television wearing Team Shearer rainbow beanies. Susie hands one to Max.

"Put it on. It's starting soon!"

Max pulls the beanie onto his head and sits in a chair. Still distracted, he keeps tapping at his laptop.

"Close that contraption and support your sister!" Dolly scolds.

"It's important!" says Max.

Dolly and Susie stare at him impatiently. Max hits one final key.

"Okay, okay, I'm done," he says. Then he shuts the lid.

On the television, a commercial for Mush Canine Cuisine concludes, and the Krumpet's Dog Show broadcast resumes.

Basil Peppercorn and Camilla Crowne-Jewel smile warmly at the camera.

"Welcome back," says Camilla. "It's the moment we've been waiting for: the final of the Agility Course Grand Championship."

"Quite right, Camilla. Ten marvelous dogs and their dedicated handlers, from all parts of the world, will be on display tonight—including the talk of the tournament, eleven-year-old Annie Shearer and Runt, all the way from Upson Downs, Australia."

"There she is!" Susie yells.

Footage of Annie's qualifying run plays onscreen. Dolly and Susie cheer and clap. Max leans forward.

"Wow," he says, staring in awe at the size of the crowd.

"A remarkable story. I imagine they will be spurring her on back at home, Basil."

And Camilla is right, because the Shearers aren't the only ones awake and watching.

At Upson Downs Primary School, students and staff and parents have gathered in the assembly hall to watch the Krumpet's Dog Show on a projection screen. There are bright streamers and balloons and signs on the walls that say Go, Annie! and Come On, Runt!

As a school project, every student has knitted their own rainbow beanie, and they wear them now. Some have taken their support a step further, digging through their own sheds at home to find tool belts as a tribute to Annie.

It warms the heart of Ms. Formsby, who wishes Annie were here to see it.

At the Golden Fleece, Mervyn Froth and his merry patrons watch on an old television set placed on the bar. They tell affectionate stories about Runt's mischievous escapades.

The cook has even prepared a special chicken schnitzel and placed it on the very table where Runt famously stole one right off the plate. They each raise a glass to Runt, behaving as though he was always their loyal and beloved friend.

"Do us proud, Runt!"

"Go on, you little ripper!"

"Bring it home, Runter!"

"He's got it in the bag. Come on, fella!"

It seems everyone in Upson Downs is watching.

There's an electricity in the air. A strange stillness. The kind of tension and excitement that makes the hair on the back of your neck stand up. A sense that something truly extraordinary is about to happen. And it is all because of Annie Shearer and Runt.

Gretel Patel sits with her family, with Bryan's rose in the corner of the room.

Even Constable Duncan Bayleaf sits in front of his television, scowling. He grips his broken snare pole, swishing it occasionally, as though he is trying to catch his nemesis through the screen.

Farther out of town, closer to the Shearers' farm, Earl Robert-Barren sits alone in his drawing room, reclining on a leather couch that once belonged to Sigmund Freud. He sips a glass of port and listens to the Krumpet's Dog Show on the BBC World Service through an antique radio. Distantly, he can hear Bryan Shearer's sheep bleating in the small pen where he has imprisoned them.

Unlike everyone else in Upson Downs, the only reason Earl is interested in the Agility Course Grand Championship is that he wants Annie Shearer to fail.

He wants Annie Shearer to fail because he wants to force the Shearers off their farm so he can buy it cheaply.

He wants to own their farm because he wants to collect all of Upson Downs.

And once he collects all of Upson Downs . . . he will move on to something else. Because Earl will never be satisfied. No matter how many artworks and artifacts he buys and hoards, or how rare and valuable they are, he will never fill the emptiness inside him.

A long way from Upson Downs, deep in the blufflands, Bernadette Box sits in her only chair with a cup of tea. She is also on her own. The single light in the room comes from her little television.

She smiles proudly when she sees Annie and Runt on the screen. She glances at the rug in front of the fireplace, where both Runt and Moxie liked to lie.

She misses her old friend.

And she realizes, quite unexpectedly, that she misses the company of her new friend too.

"Well, Camilla, all looks to be in readiness out there. The obstacle course has been immaculately prepared by the event staff. It's a sellout crowd. Absolutely perfect conditions for a wonderful contest."

"They do run a tight ship here, Basil. Hard to imagine anything at all going wrong."

"Quite right, Camilla, quite right. In fact, there has never been a single scandal or malfunction in all our years hosting the Krumpet's Dog Show, so there's simply no reason whatsoever to expect anything of the sort here this evening."

"Now, without further ado, let's cross to the arena floor. It's time for our first team to set the pace. From Paris, France, it's Harriet Snatch and her Pomeranian, Éclair."

Annie, Runt, and Bryan have returned backstage. Dozens of wall-mounted televisions display the broadcast, but Annie isn't watching, because she has noticed that the dogs around her are behaving very strangely.

They seem to be irresistibly drawn to the restricted area where the course obstacles were stored. Noses to the ground, they persistently break away from their handlers and duck under the rope, paying no heed to the **Do Not Enter** sign.

Their handlers clap their hands and call them back. Some dogs reluctantly do as they are told; others have to be collected and scolded.

Determined beagles and bloodhounds follow an invisible trail that leads them to the access corridor and toward the arena floor. They try to squeeze through the temporary fencing as though they are under a spell, and volunteers scurry about to turn them away.

Annie knows that something isn't quite right.

Trouble is brewing at the Krumpet's Dog Show.

CHAOS

Fergus Fink *has managed* to sneak his way down the access corridor and slyly observes from the sidelines.

He pays particular attention to Éclair the Pomeranian as he trots toward the starting line. Fergus is encouraged to see that the dog appears distracted. Éclair's fluffy white head twists and swivels, and his little black nose darts about.

Harriet Snatch bends and snaps her fingers in an attempt to keep her dog focused. The crowd applauds, the announcer announces, and the cameras stay trained on their subject.

Éclair makes it to the starting line. The referee nods. The officials and timekeepers are ready. The final is about to begin.

The crowd hushes.

Éclair stands poised.

Harriet Snatch waits for the chimes.

Three . . . two . . . one . . .

You may consider it odd that a dog would share the same name as a delicious pastry filled with cream, but that's likely because you don't speak French. If you did, you would know that, in France, *éclair* means *flash of lightning,* and once you saw the bright white Pomeranian zapping across the course, his name would suddenly make complete sense to you. Even more so when, just like a flash of lightning, Éclair stops as quickly as he started.

Halfway through the slalom, the mysterious temptation proves too strong. Éclair skids to a halt. He sniffs and licks the base of a pole feverishly, irrepressibly attracted to the Distilled Essence of Treat sprayed on far too thickly by Fergus Fink.

The crowd groans, disappointed for Éclair.

Harriet Snatch stands with her hands on her hips, shaking her head helplessly as the time ticks away. The referee holds up a red paddle. Their chances are dashed.

Fergus Fink smirks and chuckles to himself.

"Oh, how *very* unfortunate," laments Basil Peppercorn up in the studio.

"Such a shame. A rare display of disobedience from a very experienced competitor," says Camilla Crowne-Jewel.

Éclair doesn't care. He continues to inhale the slalom poles, deaf to Harriet's pleading. Eventually, she hooks her finger through the Pomeranian's collar and leads him away. The crowd offers a sympathetic round of applause.

The next competitor is ushered quickly through to the arena.

"Next up, we have Bob Apple from Texas and his dalmatian, Pistol. Let's hope he can post a time for us, Basil."

Bob Apple, who wears a large cowboy hat and has a belt buckle in the shape of a sheriff's badge, also senses that Pistol is distracted. He bends and leads the dalmatian swiftly to the starting line.

The referee is ready. The crowd falls silent. The three chimes sound.

Pistol is away. Bob Apple whoops and windmills his arms, and his dalmatian bounds through the slalom without issue. And for a moment, it seems all is normal again at the Krumpet's Dog Show. But disaster strikes at the entrance to the tunnel, which has been coated in Eau de Feline. Pistol stops and begins barking, then scratching, then biting, then dragging at the tube.

The crowd gasps and murmurs.

The referee flashes his red paddle.

Bob Apple throws his cowboy hat to the ground and kicks it.

Fergus Fink continues to feel smugly pleased with himself.

The officials, referee, timekeepers, television producers,

volunteers, event staff, camera operators, and members of the audience all look at each other, perplexed.

Something *very* strange is happening.

Basil Peppercorn and Camilla Crowne-Jewel are astonished and flabbergasted.

"I'm astonished," says Camilla.

"I'm flabbergasted," says Basil.

"This is the *second* competitor in as many runs who has violated the obstacles!"

"Quite right, Camilla. Unprecedented! It seems disobedience is infectious tonight."

Backstage, Bryan and Annie stare at the broadcast.

Around them, the dogs are restless and riled. They continue to run into the restricted area, rolling on their backs and rubbing their fur on the carpet. They sniff at the ground like a pack of roving vacuum cleaners. And they are intent on breaking through to the arena floor.

The only calm canine is Runt, who sits quietly between Annie's legs, already wearing his blinders.

"Geez, love, all you have to do is finish the course at this rate," says Bryan.

"Something is really wrong," says Annie. "Dogs don't just behave this way on their own."

On the course, poor Bob Apple can't seem to lure Pistol away from the tunnel. A volunteer runs over to assist.

At that moment, a rogue Jack Russell terrier called Pablo sprints into the arena, having broken free from backstage. In pursuit is Pablo's handler, Ignacio, who tries valiantly to retrieve him, but the dog is too nimble and too intent on sniffing the equipment.

The crowd gasps as a golden retriever called Mickey suddenly appears. He is joined a moment later by a Samoyed called Sputnik. They both rush toward the course, followed by their hapless handlers.

"Goodness gracious me!" Basil Peppercorn exclaims.

Then there is chaos.

A stampede of dogs pours into view, bolting from the access corridor and scattering around the arena. They attach themselves to the obstacles like a plague of locusts. They sniff and snort and roll and bark and bite and paw and lick. The crowd laughs uproariously as handlers and event staff try to round them up and restore order.

Runt is the only dog left backstage.

Annie thinks hard, looking around her, trying to put all the pieces together.

Annie snaps her fingers. She's got it.

At the same moment, a group of Very Serious People wearing matching blue blazers and gray trousers marches into the backstage area from deep within the halls of the Royal Canine Exhibition Center.

"Excuse me," says Annie, trying to get their attention.

They don't stop.

She tries again.

"Excuse me!"

They still don't stop.

"*Oi!*" Bryan shouts.

And the whole group halts and looks over at them.

There's an elderly man in the middle who wears a different, distinct jacket. It's a vintage garment, with faded red and white stripes. The man has gray hair and kind eyes. He looks familiar to Annie, but she doesn't know where she has seen him before.

"I just wanted to say . . . I think it's the obstacles," says Annie. "There's something on them that is making the dogs go crazy. I think if you clean the equipment, that should fix everything."

They all continue to stare at Annie as she approaches. Runt accompanies her, sticking close to her shins. She reaches into her tool belt and takes out a small bar of soap.

"I have this," she says, "but it's probably not enough."

The man in the red-and-white-striped jacket turns and whispers urgently to the person next to him, who nods and relays the message into a walkie-talkie. Then he bends down.

"Thank you, Annie, and thank you, Runt," he says. "I think my grandfather would have liked you both very much."

As he hastily departs with the rest of the group, Annie recalls where she has seen the man before. He looks just like the statue outside.

And for good reason, because the man is his grandson, Kingsley Krumpet the Third.

REACTIONS

In the studio, Basil and Camilla are beside themselves.

"Utterly extraordinary scenes here, Camilla! We've been overrun!"

"Sheer pandemonium! I've never seen anything like it!"

"It's a shambles! It's mayhem! Oh, my word—what is that Afghan hound doing to that seesaw? Oh, that is . . . simply *unspeakable*."

It is bedlam on the arena floor. Dogs evade being grabbed and tackled. They play tug-of-war with their leashes. They fight over the obstacles.

Fergus Fink gulps guiltily, realizing that he has clearly overdone it with the perfumes. He ducks down and creeps away, blaming Simpkins under his breath.

In Upson Downs, the Shearers can barely believe their eyes.

Dolly watches with her mouth wide open. Max grins. Susie peers at the screen, searching.

"I don't see Annie and Runt out there, do you?" she asks.

"No, I don't think so."

"Thank goodness," says Susie.

"It's like a dog park out there!" says Dolly. "They've lost control!"

"It's like a circus out there!" says Mervyn Froth, standing behind the bar at the Golden Fleece. "They've lost control!"

The pub's patrons agree with a series of nods and grunts.

In the school assembly hall, the students howl with laughter. It is, quite simply, the funniest thing they have ever seen.

Earl Robert-Barren doesn't think it's funny at all. He checks his pocket watch impatiently.

Bernadette Box is stunned. She watches with her hands on her head, leaning forward, squinting at her little television as the event staff and handlers finally round up the dogs and clear them from the floor.

The broadcast cuts back to the studio, where Basil and Camilla try to maintain their composure.

"Undoubtedly one of the most peculiar, farcical, incredible moments in Krumpet's Dog Show history."

"Quite right, Camilla. We're now being told that there will be a very brief suspension of the competition while the obstacles are thoroughly cleaned."

"Furthermore, in a show of great generosity, both Éclair

and Pistol have been granted permission to attempt their runs again, which seems fair considering these unusual circumstances."

"Quite right, Camilla. We are hearing speculation that the equipment is coated in some sort of irresistible odor. But how this has happened is anyone's guess."

"It's a mystery wrapped in a riddle, Basil. A perplexing puzzle."

"Could there be a saboteur among the competitors, Camilla? Is this a flagrant case of fragrant tampering? Something certainly smells fishy. But who could conceive of such a dastardly scheme?"

Bernadette Box leans back. Everything suddenly makes sense.

"Fergus Fink," she says to herself.

THE UNFINKABLE OCCURS

Dozens of volunteers and event staff rush out carrying disinfectant and soapy water and sponges and towels. They get to work scrubbing and rubbing and rinsing and drying.

Once they are done, a bichon frisé called Diva, who earlier in the evening won the Most Elegant Lapdog category, is brought out as a test dog.

Diva is small, white, and trimmed as neatly as a hedge. She is let loose and monitored closely by the referee and the officials. Diva struts, enjoying the adulation of the crowd, who cheers in delight as she trots about. To the relief of everyone, Diva ignores the obstacles entirely during her victory lap, pausing only once to suddenly scratch behind her ears. But with no sniffing, no licking, and no rolling, it is quickly determined that the show can resume.

And it does, without incident.

Éclair and Pistol are welcomed back to the floor, and they fly through the course, posting competitive times.

Excitement and anticipation return to the arena.

The other dogs each execute their runs without a slip or a slide or a wrong turn or a tipped hurdle or a spill from the balance beam. There isn't a single penalty awarded, and not a moment of disobedience.

The times are very close.

Pablo and Hänsel and Sputnik and Moki and Moose and Mickey all run within a tenth of a second of each other, which is the time it takes for you to blink, or for a hummingbird to flap its wings just once.

Hänsel is in the lead with a time of 37.73.

Pablo and Moki are in second and third places.

But there are still two dogs to run.

First, there is Chariot.

Then, finally, there will be Runt.

Fergus Fink is unconcerned that his Perfume Plan has gone so calamitously wrong.

When his name is called, he swaggers out to the arena floor, certain that this is the moment when he will finally fulfill his Finkdom. He will be a failure no more. He will be free. He will be famous. He will be adored.

Fergus is here to claim what he believes he is owed. He is

here to seize what the agility course community has so cruelly denied him all these years.

Victory.

And he is dressed for the occasion in his most flamboyant costume yet. Fergus wears a sparkling black-sequined jumpsuit and a matching cape with his initials imprinted on the back. The cape is lined in ruby-red silk, and it waves and billows behind him like a flag.

The crowd is astounded by his dramatic entrance. Their scattered, awkward applause doesn't give him a moment of doubt, because in his mind, the crowd is roaring for him. He waves and bows deeply, as though he is a triumphant Roman gladiator in a coliseum being showered with flowers and gifts.

He spreads his cape with both arms and slowly twirls.

Annie watches him on a screen backstage.

The way he skips about on his spindly legs with his cape spread wide and his chest puffed out reminds her of a peacock.

Some animals have hidden talents that aren't really hidden, and aren't really talents either. The peacock is one of them.

The peacock is a big bird with a bad temper that can't fly very far or run very fast. It's known for its huge, decorative tail feathers that fan out to make it appear much bigger and more impressive than it really is.

The peacock behaves this way when it wishes to intimidate or draw attention to itself, which is most of the time. And if that doesn't work, it emits a shrill call that can be heard for miles.

Fergus Fink, Annie decides, is a lot like a peacock.

And just like a peacock, Fergus is also a terrible dog handler.

While he performs for the audience, Chariot makes her way to the starting line on her own. She sits and waits.

Eventually, the referee urges Fergus to take his position. Fergus sashays into the center and poses: one arm above his head, one knee bent, like a figure skater about to begin a routine.

The crowd hushes.

Chariot crouches, staring straight ahead.

Three . . . two . . . one . . .

Chariot springs into action. She is fast and nimble. She slips through the slalom like a fish swimming downstream, then turns sharply toward the first tunnel. Her run is clean and practiced and not even remotely assisted by Fergus Fink, who twirls and leaps and flails his arms. He jabs his fingers and sweeps his hand as though he's rolling an imaginary bowling ball.

Chariot ignores him entirely. To her, Fergus Fink is just another obstacle to run around.

But she isn't without *any* guidance.

Chariot can sense Simpkins right there beside her, like a friendly phantom, urging her along and supporting her. She knows precisely what to do because of him. They have spent hours upon hours upon hours training together, preparing for this moment. And it's her loyal affection for Simpkins, the bond that they share, that gives Chariot her extraordinary focus and speed and grace.

Backstage, Annie can see it. Her eyes are glued to the screen. She feels a knot in her stomach. She knows this is a flawless run. Chariot will be very hard to beat.

Chariot whooshes through the second tunnel, expertly takes the seesaw, bounds over the last hurdle, and sprints straight for the finishing line.

"My word!" says Basil Peppercorn. "A *fantastic* run there!"

"Fergus Fink is a very . . . unusual handler, but, it must be said, this could be his year. Let's wait for the official confirmation."

On the arena floor, Fergus holds his breath and stares up at the electronic screen.

The referee raises the green paddle. No penalties.

The time flashes up for all to see.

37.52 seconds.

Chariot has seized the lead.

Fergus Fink drops dramatically to his knees, lifts his hands to the skies, and shakes his fists in triumph.

"I've done it!" he yells. "I've done it!"

At the finishing line, Chariot stands alone. She is a bit lost. She looks around nervously, unsure of what to do without her beloved friend Simpkins there to give her a pat and a dose of praise and a homemade treat.

But Simpkins is nowhere to be seen.

In fact, he didn't even watch her run.

Because Simpkins has had enough.

He is deep inside the corridors of the Royal Canine Exhibition Center, carrying a briefcase that bears the initials *FF.* Inside it are three empty perfume bottles.

Simpkins stands outside a door that leads to the Dog Show Fairness and Ethics Committee room. He is ready to do the right thing, but he is worried because he doesn't know what will happen next. He may never be able to see his dear friend Chariot again.

He takes a deep breath.

Then he knocks on the door.

THINGS THAT GO BUMP IN THE CORRIDOR

"**Miss Shearer? You're being** called through. Make your way, please."

A volunteer smiles and opens the gate for Annie and Runt to enter the access corridor.

"Are you sure I can't go in with them?" Bryan asks.

"I'm sorry, sir. Competitors only."

Bryan nods. Then he crouches down and holds Annie by the shoulders. He is jittery and excited.

"Righto, you got everything? Got your blinders on, Runt? Yep. You're good to go. Now you two go out there and enjoy it, okay? That's all that matters. All over the world, people are cheering you both on. Think of that! Go get 'em, you two. Good luck."

"We don't need luck," says Annie.

Bryan smiles and watches them step into the dim corridor.

He elbows the arm of another volunteer standing beside him, who is busy peering at a clipboard.

"That's my daughter," Bryan says.

Annie walks briskly. She can hear her name being announced. The muffled sound bounces off the walls. She can feel Runt's warm fur against her left leg. It comforts her.

Just as she nears the exit, a shadowy figure suddenly appears and collides with her. Annie staggers backward. The person trips and falls to the ground, briefly tangling with Runt, then quickly stands up.

It is Fergus Fink, with Chariot trailing behind.

Annie steels herself, but his tone is unusually kind and concerned.

"Goodness me, I'm so sorry, Annie. We really must stop bumping into each other. Though the last time this happened, I got a free pie for my troubles! Are you hurt?"

"I'm fine," says Annie.

"Good, good. Listen, I want to wish you both well out there. You're a worthy adversary, and I underestimated you. May the best dog win."

Annie frowns and straightens her beanie.

"Okay. Thank you," she says.

Fergus smiles and sweeps his cape back, continuing down the corridor.

Annie rattles her head, dazed from the bump and confused by Fergus Fink's sudden warmth. Maybe he's changed for the better, she thinks. Maybe she has underestimated him too.

Annie steps out into the arena. The noise of the crowd hits her so powerfully that she feels as though she is floating. Thousands of eyes stare at her, and the cameras follow her path across the course to the starting line. Annie looks straight ahead, her chin held high.

The referee and the officials and the timekeepers and the volunteers all watch them. Kingsley Krumpet the Third and his team look on from a special box in the front row.

"And here they are," says Camilla Crowne-Jewel in the studio. "The underdogs of Upson Downs. It's eleven-year-old Annie Shearer and the stray dog Runt, all the way from Down Under."

And in Upson Downs, Down Under, the Shearers are up on their feet, hooting and hollering and waving their arms.

"There she is!" yells Dolly. "There's our Annie!"

In the school assembly hall, the students roar into life. They leap out of their seats and wave their rainbow beanies in the air. The staff and parents laugh and clap.

In the Golden Fleece, they each raise a glass and toast Runt and Annie Shearer. They slap the bar and shout like it's a football match.

The whole town has been brought together, connected by a little girl and her dog. In all the homes of Upson Downs, there is hope and there is happiness. There is a mysterious energy in the air. A strange force that makes the night feel alive in a way that it hasn't for a very long time.

Something is stirring. Something momentous.

Even Earl Robert-Barren can sense it.

He sits up straight, sniffing, listening, looking over his shoulder.

Outside the manor, the sheep bleat in a loud chorus from their pen. The horses whinny and gallop up and down the fence line. Kangaroos thump the dirt as they hop away. Boobook owls call eerily from the branches.

Earl gets to his feet. He lights an old oil lantern that once belonged to the polar explorer Ernest Shackleton.

He stands at his front door and peers into the darkness.

"Is anyone out there?"

His voice wavers, bearing none of his usual bombastic bullying. He listens but receives no response.

Earl is entirely alone.

Bernadette Box feels tingles down her neck when she sees Annie stride across the floor. She smiles, blushing with pride.

Then she notices that something doesn't appear quite right. Bernadette squints at the television. She gasps and brings her hand to her mouth.

Many miles away, Susie has seen it too.

She stops cheering and goes very still.

"Oh no," she says.

THE BIG MOMENT

Annie reaches the starting line, and for the first time since entering the arena, she looks down at Runt.

And that's when *she* sees it.

Her eyes widen with panic.

Her stomach drops and twists.

At the same moment, Fergus Fink, his hands hidden by his cape, approaches a rubbish bin backstage. With his smuggest, slyest smile, he secretly discards a very important item.

His collision with Annie Shearer was no accident. It was carefully planned and executed. As he toppled to the ground, Fergus covered Runt with his cape and stripped off his blinders with the skill of a pickpocket.

And now he has thrown them away.

But Annie isn't aware of that. All she knows is that, at the worst possible time, Runt isn't wearing them. Her heart and mind are racing. Did she forget? She was *certain* he'd had them on. Maybe he shook them off, which means they might still be backstage, or in the access corridor. She looks over her shoulder. Maybe she can run and look for them. Maybe there's still time. Maybe she can still fix it.

"Take your position, please!" the referee calls out.

Annie is frozen in place.

"An interesting development here, Camilla. Young Annie appears to have decided against employing the blinders for the final."

"Perhaps she's feeling confident that Runt is comfortable on the big stage?"

"Quite a risk, Camilla. But given he must run faster than 37.52 seconds, I suppose now is not the time to be coy."

"There appears to be a problem, Basil. Perhaps this wasn't a strategic choice after all. . . ."

In the lounge room, Susie gestures wildly.

"She's forgotten them! I knew this would happen! Bryan Shearer, you pumpkin of a man, you had *one* job! I told him, *Make sure she doesn't forget those blinders before she goes out there!* And now look!"

Bryan, watching the screen backstage, slaps his forehead.

"Oh no," he says to himself. "Susie is going to make pies out of me. It makes no sense. I was *sure* he had them on."

He looks around frantically. The blinders must have slipped off somehow. If he can find them quickly, he might be able to run them out in time. He searches under dog beds and crates and tables and boxes and bags but comes up with nothing.

Annie turns to the referee.

"He's not wearing his blinders," she says. "Can I go back and get them, please?"

The referee shakes his head.

"I'm afraid not. Leaving the course is an automatic disqualification. Please take your position."

Annie is out of options.

She drops to one knee.

She cups her hands around Runt's eyes and brings her face close to his so that she is all he can see.

"You can do this, Runt. You can block them all out. You just . . . *have* to. *Please.* It's for our home. It's for the overdraft on the overdraft. And it's for all those people who gave us a little bit of what they have so that we could be here. Nobody wants to chase you or catch you or lock you up anymore. They really like you, Runt. It's just a few seconds for us right now, but it will mean everything for every minute and every hour and every day that comes after."

"Take. Your. Position! Final warning!"

The referee sounds stern.

Annie retreats, keeping her eyes on Runt.

She finds her mark.

The crowd falls silent.

In the lounge room, the Shearers do too. So does everyone in the school assembly hall, the Golden Fleece, and every home in Upson Downs. Bernadette Box watches between her fingers. Bryan stops searching and stares at the screen backstage, his big chest rising and falling.

"Come on, Runt," he says.

This is the moment.

Annie lifts her magic finger toward the roof. Her knees feel rubbery. But she is ready.

Annie looks at Runt. Runt looks at Annie.

"Please," she whispers.

She waits for the chimes.

Three . . .

Two . . .

One . . .

"Come on, Runt! Come on! Let's go! Let's *go!*"

Annie sweeps her arm and points her magic finger. The crowd erupts.

But Runt doesn't move.

"Please, Runt! *Please!* Come on through! You can do it! Come on!"

She waves at him, yelling as loud as she can.

But Runt doesn't move.

The crowd groans in sympathy.

Annie is heavy with dread and disappointment, but she can't bring herself to give up.

I can still fix this, she thinks.

Desperate and determined, Annie rushes over to the starting line. She bends down and scoops Runt up into her arms, and she carries him onto the course, running and stumbling awkwardly. The crowd is stunned. They murmur and whisper as she weaves her way between the slalom poles. Behind her, the referee holds up his red paddle. Annie has committed a number of disqualifying penalties. But that won't stop her. She clambers over a high jump, tipping the bar.

The audience urges her on.

"Go on, Annie!"

"You can do it!"

They yell and clap and whistle. But Annie can barely hear them. She's still racing the clock, going as fast as her legs will carry her.

"What a brave and brilliant young girl," says Camilla.

"Absolutely right, Camilla. Absolutely right."

All across Upson Downs, the reactions are the same. First they were deflated, then they were surprised, and now they are inspired.

As the onlookers watch her carry her dog, they are proud to know Annie Shearer. And all around them, the air grows thicker and suddenly colder. It seems to crackle and buzz with a static charge. A hidden force builds and builds, like a bowstring being drawn farther and farther back.

And in the farmhouse, Susie Shearer is standing with her hand on her heart, yelling at the television, bursting with emotion.

"For goodness' sake, Bryan! Go out there and help her!"

And at that precise moment, on the other side of the planet, Bryan Shearer jolts into action, as though he has just heard Susie's appeal.

He bulldozes through the access corridor gate, pushing past the volunteers and event staff who try to stop him.

"Out of my way! That's my daughter!"

Bryan bustles and barges and hustles and hurries out onto the arena floor.

The referee is shaking his red paddle so furiously that his face is beginning to match its color.

Bryan catches up with Annie just as she reaches the entrance of the first tunnel. Annie stops and looks up at him, still clutching Runt to her chest. She knows it's all over. She has failed.

"We couldn't do it," she says. "We didn't win."

Bryan kneels down and puts his arm around her.

"It's okay, love. It doesn't matter. It's okay."

Annie lowers Runt down. The whole stadium is completely still.

"I just wanted . . . ," she says hopelessly. "I just wanted to . . ."

Then, for the first time in her life, in front of the whole world, Annie Shearer begins to cry. Bryan pulls her in and holds her close. Worried, Runt sniffs at her ankle, then gives her hand a supportive lick.

A tear drips off Annie's chin and hits the ground.

Splat.

THE MIRACLE

Splat. Splat.

"Do you hear that?" asks Max Shearer in Upson Downs.

Susie and Dolly are both watching Bryan and Annie on the television. They are so overcome with love that they don't even hear Max's question, let alone any odd noises.

Splat. Tink. Plink. Clap.

Max looks up and around.

"What *is* that?"

Driven by curiosity, Max steps outside.

The air is still and dense and eerily cold. It smells strangely sweet.

He hears a faint squeaking whir over by the windmill. Barefoot, in his pajamas, he walks over to inspect it. His hair stands on end, as though he is being sucked into the sky.

He tilts his head back and looks up. His mouth drops open.

Though the blades of the windmill are perfectly still, the Rainmaker is spinning as fast as a propeller. It rattles and shakes as though it might work loose at any moment and fizz off into the night.

Beyond it, distantly, a big fat foreboding cloud has formed, blocking out every star and bathing the night in shadow.

And watching that black cloud, Max witnesses a spectacular phenomenon. There are flares and flashes of white. And then a deep, loud, rolling rumble that makes the ground tremor and his legs shake and his broken bone ache.

For the first time in his life, Max Shearer feels a ripple of fear.

Splat.

Something hits him in the eye.

He blinks hard and wipes it away. It's wet. He licks his hand, and then he gasps.

"It worked," he whispers.

Inside, Susie and Dolly hug each other with tears in their eyes. They watch as Annie takes Bryan's hand and leads him off the arena floor. They can see how the crowd rises to their feet to show their respect, clapping for Annie and Runt.

"They're cheering for you, Annie," says Dolly with a smile. "Because you're so brave."

The sound of the clapping gets louder and louder, until it's quite deafening.

"They're so loud!" Susie shouts.

"Turn the telly down!"

Susie points the remote control and lowers the volume, but the applause remains. They look at each other, confused.

Then they look up at the roof.

Susie and Dolly rush outside. They hold their palms out and look up at the night sky.

Fat, sparse drops of rain spatter their hands and thud into the dusty ground around them.

Max runs over to them. His face is slick with moisture, his pajamas dotted with droplets.

"She did it!" he says. "I don't know how, but she did it!"

He points up at the Rainmaker, and just as he does so, a thin blue bolt of lightning zaps the contraption, and there is a splash of sparks like fireworks. A second later, there is a boom as loud as a dozen cannons.

The Shearers duck and pull their rainbow beanies down over their ears, looking up in terror and awe. Max stares at his pointing finger, as though he is Thor himself.

Then there is silence.

The Rainmaker has been incinerated into a charred husk. Bits of metal are strewn across the dirt.

And the raindrops abruptly stop.

The Shearers straighten and catch their breath, long enough to feel disappointed that it's all over already.

"What on earth was all tha—"

Boom!

Dolly is interrupted by another blast of thunder.

And with it, the skies are torn open.

It *pours* with rain.

All over Upson Downs, people run outside to greet the storm. They shriek and laugh and dance in the deluge.

Fresh water pools and streams around their feet. They jump and splash, they grin and giggle. Couples waltz in the rain. Others hoot and holler and jig. Some open their mouths and drink it straight from the sky. The rain is so precious that they collect it in buckets and fill their water tanks by hand.

Claudia Velour takes the opportunity to wash her hair.

Fiona Grudge has her first shower in three months.

Harold Croydon washes his beloved Mercedes in his driveway.

Students play on the school oval, slipping and sliding in the slick mud.

The cracks in the parched creek beds fill and come to life.

And still the rain pours down. There is joy and relief in Upson Downs.

At every single address except one.

DAM

Earl Robert-Barren glares out the window of his manor, his hands balled into fists.

The storm is torrential.

Earl knows that a flash flood could cause the water to rise and pour over the dirt banks of his dam wall. And if that happens, the structure might crumble and break and all his hoarded water would spill down the hill and fill the rivers and creeks and gulches and water holes of the town and farms below, relieving the pressure he has put them under and making their land harder to collect.

And Earl can't have that.

Fuming, he strides urgently to his wardrobe and hurries into a yellow raincoat and gum boots that he has never had cause to wear.

Carrying Shackleton's lantern, he trudges out into the

storm, squinting as the rain smacks him in the face. The ground is slippery. He slides and stumbles.

With great annoyance, he sees that Bryan Shearer's sheep have forced open a gap in their pen and are escaping. Earl waves his arms and attempts to block their path, but they dart around him and scatter into the night.

One spooked ewe puts her head down and charges squarely into his stomach. Earl staggers and falls, the wind knocked out of him. He clambers to his feet, gasping for breath. The lantern's flame gutters and flickers. By the time he reaches the pen to repair the breach, the last sheep has gone.

Miserable, and cursing under his breath, Earl stomps and clomps up the slope of his property, battered by the driving rain, pausing often to catch his breath.

Finally he reaches the muddy wall of his dam.

He begins climbing, but the soil is loose and as slick as oil. He can't get any grip with his gum boots, which have filled with water and weigh him down like twin anchors.

So Earl crawls up on his hands and knees, groaning with effort.

When he reaches the top of the wall, his fears are confirmed. The dam is so full that water is spilling over, taking dirt and sand and rocks with it. Desperate, Earl tries to scrape the mud back into place with his hands, but the rushing water is too strong, and growing more powerful by the moment.

Earl drops the lantern, and it is carried away. Shrouded in darkness, he stubbornly persists in trying to hold his wall together. He crouches like a greedy grizzly bear in a rushing stream. But Earl is not trying to snatch salmon. He is trying to catch the river.

Around him, the wall crumbles. Huge chunks break loose and are stolen by the current. The wall gets weaker as the flow gains force. Earl is sinking. Water rushes at him, and he struggles to hold on.

Then, beneath him and around him, the whole structure splits and gives way. Earl is suddenly powerless and weightless as a great wave bursts free and swallows him whole, and he realizes, all too late, that nature has no owners.

Earl himself has been collected by his biggest prize. He is swept along as the vast dam empties itself, the water surging down the hillsides and slopes and gullies and back into the riverbeds and creeks where it belongs.

THE WINNER

And still it rains.

Susie, Max, and Dolly squelch their way back inside the farmhouse, sopping wet.

They are so surprised and elated by the deluge that they have altogether forgotten about Annie's disappointment in London, but on the television, the award ceremony is being broadcast. Kingsley Krumpet the Third hands the Grand Championship Cup to Fergus Fink, who snatches it eagerly and lifts it above his head. He laughs maniacally. Neither Chariot nor Simpkins has joined him on the podium.

"Look at this twinkling germ," Dolly sneers.

The crowd has not stayed to applaud Fergus Fink, but that doesn't stop him from enthusiastically celebrating himself. He digs into his own pocket and tosses handfuls of his own confetti into the air.

"A long-awaited victory for Fergus Fink, Basil."

"Quite right, Camilla. And doesn't he look pleased with himself."

"Very. Though, it must be said, on a truly eventful evening here at the Krumpet's Dog Show, our hearts have been stolen by another team from Down Under."

The dignitaries and officials and event staff drift away. A volunteer politely encourages Fergus to leave the podium, but he won't budge.

Max, meanwhile, has dried himself off and opened his laptop. He can bear the temptation no longer. He taps a few keys, waits a moment, then stares at the screen in disbelief.

He blinks hard.

"Whoa," he says quietly.

Susie twists around and looks at him suspiciously.

"What have you done now?"

ONE MAN'S TRASH

Backstage, Annie and Bryan are dejected. Runt sticks close to Annie's shins, protective and concerned.

Around them, handlers and staff are packing up and preparing to leave. Dogs snooze in their crates. Tables are folded up. Bags are zipped.

"Can we go?" Annie asks.

Bryan nods.

"You got everything?" he asks.

"Everything except Runt's blinders," Annie says.

They head toward the exit. As they walk past, other competitors offer Annie encouraging words of sympathy and support.

They reach the sliding doors. Bryan touches the pass on his lanyard to the screener, and the doors open.

And there, crowded in the lobby, are the journalists and

photographers who would ordinarily have been on the arena floor to speak to the winner. They are all waiting for Annie Shearer.

"There she is!" a reporter shouts.

The media begin pressing forward, pointing microphones and recorders and cameras. They jostle for position and all call out at once.

"Annie, can I have a moment to speak with you?"

"Miss Shearer! Roger Bean here from the *Canine Inquirer*. There's been quite a response to your—"

"Annie! What happened to the blinders? Were you threatened with disqualification behind the scenes?"

"Audrey Foot, Radio Six. There are rumors of potential foul play with the equipment tonight. Do you care to comment?"

"Annie! The whole world is reacting to your—"

Bryan steps forward to shield his daughter.

"Righto, steady on, you lot! That's enough."

Annie hurriedly dabs her own pass against the screener, and they retreat back through the doors.

"How do we get out of here?" asks Bryan.

Annie kneels to make sure Runt isn't frightened or agitated.

"Let's see if there's another way," she says.

They return to the backstage area and scan for other exits.

Annie points.

"Over there! Look!"

An elderly man in a cleaner's uniform is picking up rubbish bins and lifting them onto a small trailer attached to an electric cart. He hops in and drives deeper into the exhibition center.

"Quick!" says Annie. "Let's follow him."

They hurry after the cart through passageways and thoroughfares, struggling to keep up. Annie's tool belt flaps against her legs. Bryan is red-faced and out of breath.

They almost lose track of the little vehicle, chasing it all the way to a large roller door.

They run through it and find themselves on a loading dock outside the center.

Here it is dark and quiet. There are no reporters or photographers.

The cleaner parks the cart beside a huge metal bin. Slowly, and with great effort, he lifts a smaller rubbish bin from the trailer and empties it into the larger container.

Bryan, still puffing, approaches him.

"Let me give you a hand with those," he says.

The old man startles.

"Blimey, you've almost made my heart pop! Didn't see you there. Are you lost?"

"No, mate."

Bryan puts a comforting hand on the old man's shoulder and leads him to the cart.

"Come on, you have a seat. I'll take care of these."

"Thank you, lad," says the old man. "It's been a long day."

Seeing the two of them together makes Annie think of Grandpa Wally. She smiles, but she feels sad too.

Annie steps forward to help with the rubbish bins. Bryan lifts and empties them one by one, and Annie returns them to the trailer. Runt lends his assistance by devouring a fallen hot dog bun.

As Bryan lifts the last bin, Annie glimpses something.

"Wait!"

Bryan puts it down and Annie peers inside. She reaches in and removes Runt's blinders.

Bryan stares with his mouth open.

"How did they end up in there?"

"Wasn't me," says the old man.

"It must have been *someone*," says Bryan.

Annie thinks back to the hard bump in the access corridor, the strange fumbling, Fergus Fink's sudden kindness.

It all makes sense.

"I think I know," she says. "But it's too late now."

"I'm really sorry, love," says Bryan.

Annie puts the blinders in the biggest pocket of her tool belt. As she does so, she feels a folded square of paper wedged in the corner. Curious, she takes it out and immediately remembers. It's Grandpa Wally's last diary entry, the one she tore from his journal.

"What's that?" Bryan asks.

Annie can't answer.

Bryan looks concerned.

"Annie, are you all right?"

Then Annie has an idea. Perhaps her best one yet.

"There's somewhere I think you should see before we go back home. It's not on the itinerary, but I read about it. It's not very far from here."

Bryan nods.

"Righto. Lead the way," he says.

EMERALD CITY

Kew Gardens is home to the world's largest botanical collection.

There are over fifty *thousand* different species of plants from all over the world on display.

And it's where Annie Shearer has brought her father.

They stroll along the paths in the bright silver moonlight. Beyond the dewy carpet of grass there are oak trees, cedars, junipers, black walnuts, giant redwoods, and weeping beeches. They walk past perfectly manicured beds of tulips, roses, lavenders, and orchids and a pond of water lilies. The air is cool and sweetly perfumed. Frogs *bwark* and crickets *preep*. They have the entire garden to themselves. The grounds are so tranquil and still that it feels like they're in a paddock at home, not in the middle of a city.

Annie stops at a fork in the path. She looks both ways and makes a quick estimation.

"It's down here," she says, leading them to the left.

"What is?"

"You'll see."

They soon step down a paved lane with rows of blossoming apple trees on either side.

Then Bryan sees it.

He halts as though he's walked into a wall. He is utterly spellbound.

"Oh, Annie. It's *incredible.*"

Standing before him is an enormous greenhouse, twenty meters high and larger than an airplane hangar.

"It's called the Temperate House," Annie explains as they make their way toward the entrance. "It's over a hundred and fifty years old. When it was built, it was the biggest greenhouse in the whole world. It took over forty years to make it, and there are fifteen thousand panes of glass. I read about it."

Bryan stares up at the architectural marvel. Its wrought-iron skeleton is grand and ornate, and the thick glass panes gleam emerald.

"You reckon it's bigger than mine at home?"

Annie smiles and pretends to consider it.

"Maybe a little bit. We'd have to measure it."

"Yeah, maybe just a little bit."

"There are over ten thousand different plants inside," says Annie.

"Really?"

"Really really."

Bryan whistles, shaking his head in awe.

Tempted, he looks left, then he looks right. And he steps forward to test the brass doorknob on the old doors of the entrance.

But sadly, they are locked.

"Ah, well," says Bryan, stepping back. "Worth a shot, eh? Another time."

The entrance doors are as old as the rest of the building. Annie peers at the keyhole. It has a strange shape, which gives her an idea.

She fumbles around in her tool belt and takes out the old key she fished out of the canal.

Annie feels bashful and a bit silly, because it's absurd to think that of all the locks in London, this key could be the one to fit.

Still, she is strangely hopeful. The key seems to glow warm in her hand.

She knows it can't possibly work, but her heart thumps fast as she feeds it into the keyhole.

She twists it.

It doesn't turn.

She jiggles it, and the key shunts farther down the cavity, fitting snugly. She tries again.

Click.

The lock turns.

Annie and Bryan stare at each other with wide eyes.

"I'll be honest with you," says Bryan. "I didn't expect that."

"Neither did I. Should we go in? We might get in trouble."

"Come on," whispers Bryan. "A quick gander can't hurt. What are they gonna do, kick us out of the country?"

The two slip inside, with Runt trotting alongside them.

They pass through the foyer into an expansive central atrium. It's a breathtaking glass cathedral, and inside it grows an extraordinary garden. They walk down a neat path with thick forest on either side. There are palm trees and ferns and a smorgasbord of shrubs. Bryan is awestruck by the size and variety of plants growing in harmony. It is a world of wonder. He is walking through paradise.

"Look! A trumpet vine! They're from Africa. Oh, bush lilies! Pincushions. Here's a tea plant. Pomegranate. And these bellflowers, aren't they gorgeous? They're so delicate." He gasps. "Oh, and have a squiz at this!"

He kneels and points to a huge spiky flower.

"A golden lotus banana," he says excitedly, sniffing it. "What a ripper. I've never seen one. It smells delicious!"

"That's a banana?"

"Distant relative," answers Bryan. "Whether you're a Shearer or a banana, one family can have a lot of different varieties."

They wander past a tall spiral staircase that leads up to a viewing area. Eventually, they reach the very middle of the greenhouse and take a seat on a bench.

Bryan perches on the edge, looking up and around, truly at a loss for words.

Annie watches Runt. He looks relaxed and content, and her thoughts drift back to the race. Her shoulders slump as her disappointment creeps back.

"I really thought he was going to do it with everyone watching," she says quietly. "Even without the blinders on, I really thought he would run and we would win."

Bryan rubs her back.

"I'm sorry, mate."

They watch Runt sniff about curiously. Bryan has a thought.

"Maybe we can keep looking for a special coach or a trainer when we're back home, and we can try again next year. I'll call around. We'll get the best there is, see if they can help fix him."

Annie shakes her head.

"He doesn't need fixing. He's not broken. He's just . . . Runt. And there's nothing wrong with that. That's what Bernadette Box was trying to tell me, but I didn't listen properly because I wanted to win so bad. She never made it here to London because her dog, Moxie, hated traveling in those little crates. And Bernadette didn't try to force her, or to find a way around it. She just accepted it. Moxie was more important to her than winning. Bernadette said she couldn't ask Moxie to be someone she wasn't. But that's what I did with Runt. I was asking him to be someone he's not. And it wasn't fair for me to do that. The worst thing is, it was all for nothing."

"Nothing? *Nothing?* Annie Shearer, think about how far you've come. You two are *national champions* who made the final at the Krumpet's Dog Show. That isn't nothing. That's amazing."

"But I didn't win. I didn't fix anything. Now we can't pay for the overdraft on the overdraft, and we can't pay Mr. Robert-Barren either, and we will have to leave Upson Downs."

Bryan takes a deep breath.

"Is that what this has all been about? Annie, that's not your burden. It's mine and your mum's. It's our duty and our honor to make sure you and your brother and Grandma Dolly are safe and happy and healthy, wherever we live. Listen, you are a thoughtful, clever, selfless person, and it's a wonderful way to be. But you don't have to carry the weight of the world in your tool belt. And you don't need to fix *everything*. Because if you're too busy looking for things to fix, all you ever see are problems, and you miss out on the stuff that already works. I mean, look at where we are. Look at where you've taken us. Annie, this might be the most extraordinary place I have ever been in my whole life. I feel like I'm in a dream. I don't want to think about all those problems at home. I just want to sit here and share all this beauty with you."

Bryan leans forward and plucks a primrose. He hands it to her.

"Sometimes you've got to stop and smell the flowers. You know, you remind me so much of your grandpa Wally, it's downright spooky. And I wish . . ."

Bryan clears his throat. "I wish I'd said the same thing to him."

Annie sits quietly for a moment.

"He knew," she says. "And he wishes he said some things to you too."

Bryan nods, but he doesn't reply.

Annie feels that folded square of paper burning a hole in her tool belt. She fishes it out and gives it to him.

"What's this?" he asks as he unfolds the paper.

"It's from Grandpa Wally."

Bryan's hands are trembling slightly.

"It's too dark in here for me to see," he whispers. "You read it."

And she does.

By moonlight, inside the great greenhouse, Annie reads Wally Shearer's last diary entry out loud. And Wally gets to speak to Bryan one last time.

"He's a good man and a good son, but he deserves to walk his own path. Everyone does."

When Annie looks up, she sees that her dad is crying, but he doesn't look sad or upset. She has never seen him cry before, and she doesn't quite know what to do or what to say or how to fix it.

She reaches out and holds his big hand.

They sit together and share the silence.

"You know, Annie," Bryan says finally, "I think I've been asking myself to be someone I'm not for a long time. And that's not fair either."

He wraps his arms around his daughter and gives her a big hug.

"Thank you," he says.

Bryan's pocket starts to buzz. His phone, which has been on silent all night, is vibrating. He digs it out.

"It's your mother. Blow me down, I've missed thirty calls. I should probably answer this one—what do you reckon?"

"I hope they're not too upset."

Bryan accepts the video chat.

Susie, Dolly, and Max have all squeezed into view. Their hair is wet, and to Annie's surprise, they are grinning.

"Why are you all drenched?" asks Bryan.

"It's *raining*!" they yell at once.

"What?"

"It worked, Annie!" says Max. "The Rainmaker worked! You made a whole storm!"

Bryan looks at Annie.

"What is he talking about?"

"Is it really raining?" Annie asks. "Or is this a Kind Lie?"

"It's smashing down!" says Dolly. "Never seen anything like it. The water tank's full already!"

"The whole district has been soaked," says Susie. "It's a miracle!"

"But that's not even everything," says Max proudly. He holds up his laptop. "Annie, you've gone viral!"

"What does that mean?" Bryan asks, suddenly concerned.

He presses his hand to Annie's forehead, checking her temperature. "Is she going to be okay?"

"Not *that* kind of viral, you biscuit," says Dolly. "Computer viral."

"I'm a bit confused," says Annie.

So her brother explains.

HIDDEN TALENTS

The truth is, Max Shearer has been busy.

Since he broke his arm at the Woolarama Show and was made to stay indoors, Max has been secretly filming.

At first, he started recording because he was bored. After a while, he enjoyed the small thrill of capturing private moments without being detected. It wasn't quite the same rush as leaping off a hundred-foot pole, but it soon became an obsession.

He filmed Annie and Runt training in their scrapyard course and was amazed by the tricks and stunts Runt could perform when he thought nobody was watching. He filmed Runt expertly herding the sheep. He filmed Runt devouring Mush Canine Cuisine, and he recorded the stack of empty dog food tins. He filmed Runt resting his head on Annie's lap. He filmed Runt following Annie wherever she went. He filmed Runt's triumph at the National Titles, and he filmed him bolting from the building.

He filmed other things too:

Bryan getting stuck in his leather jacket.

Earl Robert-Barren at the door, threatening their farm.

The dry, cracked creek beds of Upson Downs. The vacant homes and farms and stores. The empty railway station. The dilapidated Big Ram. The **For Sale** signs.

The fundraising to get Annie and Runt to London.

Susie knitting their rainbow beanies.

The only thing he didn't film was himself.

Max Shearer captured hundreds of moments. And he wasn't sure why, until it occurred to him that he could stitch them all together to tell a true tale. A story about his sister and the remarkable Runt. A film about his family, about Upson Downs and all the people in it.

It took days to edit and assemble. And just before Annie and Runt made their appearance in the final of the Krumpet's Dog Show, he posted the video to his YouTube channel for everyone to see.

Other than Runt's stunts, the video didn't boast any spectacular feats or death-defying acts or daredevilry, so Max didn't think anyone would be interested. But he had worked really hard and put his heart into it, so he hoped a few people might notice.

In his wildest dreams, Max could not have imagined what happened next.

"*How* many people have watched it?" Annie asks.

"Ten *million*," Max repeats. "And it's only been a couple of hours. My notifications are off the hook. It's being reposted *everywhere*. It just keeps going!"

"And that's not all," says Dolly.

"The phone hasn't stopped ringing," says Susie. "Television, radio, newspapers from all over the world—Sweden and Argentina and Korea and Zimbabwe. They all want to speak to you, Annie! Everyone loves you and Runt, and they want to talk about what happened tonight."

"But there's something even *bigger* than that!" says Dolly, who looks ready to burst.

"What?" says Bryan.

Susie takes a deep breath.

"We just got a message from a man called Angus Franklin, the head of Mush Canine Cuisine worldwide. He was there at the final tonight, and he also watched Max's video. And he is asking Runt to be the exclusive face of Mush Canine Cuisine. He wants Runt featured on the label, and he wants Runt to do commercials and conventions and public appearances and all sorts of other things. He's offering Runt a lifetime supply of Mush, and for Annie . . ."

Susie trails off, quite overcome.

"He's offering a lot of money," she finishes.

"Enough for the overdraft on the overdraft?" Annie asks quietly.

Susie nods.

Bryan looks at Annie, who is stunned and at a loss for words.

"We might have to call you back," he says.

"Of course," says Susie.

"We love you, Annie!" says Dolly.

"We're so proud of you!" says Susie.

The phone screen goes black.

They are in the darkness again. When his eyes adjust, Bryan sees that Runt is sitting at Annie's feet, looking up at her attentively, unaware that he is the most famous dog in the world.

"Well, Runt," he says. "You might have to get used to people looking at you."

Annie's mind is swirling.

It's hard to believe that while she sits peacefully in a giant greenhouse in London, it is raining in Upson Downs, their farm is safe, people all over the world know who she is, and Runt can have all the Mush Canine Cuisine he could ever eat.

The thought that Annie keeps returning to is how everybody helped in their own way by using their own hidden talents.

Maybe her dad was right. Maybe she didn't need to try to fix everything on her own. And besides, it was much more fun to be part of Team Shearer, working together.

She thinks about Grandpa Wally and his biggest regret: that he didn't spend more time with the people he loved.

Annie stands up.

There is one last thing to fix.

She reaches behind her, unclips her worn leather tool belt, and takes it off. She feels much lighter without it.

She hands it to her father.

"I don't need this anymore," says Annie Shearer.

UPSON DOWNS AND UP AGAIN

Very quickly, everything changes.

The rain stops in Upson Downs, but the river and creeks remain full and flowing. Green shoots emerge from the soil. The wildflowers and wildlife return.

And so too do the people.

Mystery surrounds the disappearance of Earl Robert-Barren. He hasn't been seen since the night of the storm. Constable Duncan Bayleaf searches the area and questions the locals, but nobody knows the circumstances behind Earl's sudden vanishing.

As time passes, Earl falls behind on the taxes and council rates for his estate and his many properties. His debts grow larger and larger. Since Earl has no family, no friends, no will and testament, and no legal representation, the shire of

Upson Downs has no choice but to assume ownership of his estate and his collection of farms.

At a town meeting, the locals of Upson Downs vote unanimously to invite people back to their properties.

To pay for the maintenance of Earl's vast estate, it is agreed that his manor and his private collection should be turned into a museum and opened to the public. Every priceless painting, every rare trinket, every historic artifact, every book, every musical instrument, every ornament, every jewel is put on display. They can be seen and appreciated by anyone who wishes to visit.

After being hoarded and hidden for so long, Earl's collection quickly gains a reputation as one of the most remarkable and valuable in the entire world. The museum becomes an unmissable tourist destination. People travel from all over the globe to traipse through his house, marveling at the extraordinary exhibition.

Having fallen off the map, Upson Downs gets back up again.

The railway station is refurbished. The town hall is reopened. The main street is bustling and busy. Business booms, and not a single shop is empty. There are cafés, restaurants, bookstores, beauty parlors, hardware stores, and banks. And one shop in particular proves so popular that it becomes a drawcard in its own right.

It belongs to Susie Shearer.

The shop is called Humble Pie, but to the relief of all, including Susie, there is no pastry, no filling, and no food for sale.

Susie always suspected that her pies were awful, but she was so encouraged by the Kind Lies of her family that she doubted her own sense of taste. It turned out the only person who ever told the truth about them was Annie.

Now that she no longer has to scour the supermarket for bargains to keep them all fed, Susie finally admits that she really dislikes cooking. She vows never to make another pie, or even set foot in the kitchen.

And besides, she is far too busy doing what she loves, because Humble Pie is the name of Susie Shearer's clothing label.

Making blinders out of Bryan's old leather jacket reminded her of how much she enjoyed sewing and constructing. So she turned her attention to the racks and stacks of vintage clothes she had stored away. Now she snips and trims and sews and joins and turns old garments into modern fashions. Her shop is full of outfits that she has reimagined and redesigned. Every piece is completely unique, and she can barely keep up with the demand.

Some visitors fall in love with Upson Downs and never leave. The town swells in size.

The cricket club, the football club, the tennis club, the golf club, the bowls club, the badminton club, the bridge club, the darts club, the boxing gym, the amateur theater, the choir, and the dance hall all reopen, and Dolly Shearer is declared president of them all. It makes her happy to be busy and social and competitive again.

But there's something missing.

Dolly Shearer is still looking for love.

The Big Ram is given a fresh coat of paint, and its broken horn and its bung eye are repaired. It stands proud as a cloud, but there's a more recent landmark in Upson Downs that attracts a bigger crowd.

It's a statue, right beside the Big Ram, and it's much, much smaller.

In fact, it's life-size.

It's a dog called Runt, cast in bronze and sitting perfectly still, as he always does when people are watching.

And just like with Gorgeous George, it's considered a gesture of luck and great fortune to place a hand over Runt's heart.

Among the first visitors to Runt's statue is Constable Duncan Bayleaf. Humbly, he lays his broken snare pole at the foot of the monument and retires it forever, finally conceding defeat.

Another familiar face arrives to pay his respects and to make amends.

Instead of offering a snare pole, the man places two fake eyebrows and a fake mustache at the base of the statue.

It is Simpkins, who bows deeply and apologizes to Runt and Annie Shearer, even though they're not there to hear him.

Simpkins is no longer employed by Fergus Fink, and the truth is, nobody ever will be again.

Back in London, after Simpkins handed over the briefcase with the offending perfumes and explained what Fergus had done, the Krumpet's Dog Show Fairness and Ethics Committee acted swiftly.

Fergus wasn't able to celebrate his victory for long. The moment he stepped away from the podium, he was briskly led into the Chamber of Judgment. Kingsley Krumpet the Third himself delivered the verdict. Fergus Fink was charged with Course Tampering, Competitive Sabotage, and Conduct Unbecoming a Handler. Convicted on all counts, Fergus Fink was stripped of his Grand Championship title and banned from ever again competing in any event involving canines or agility.

Fergus ranted. He raved. He argued. He denied. He begged. He threatened legal action. He stomped his foot and shook his fists. He declared himself the victim of a cruel conspiracy. He even tried to flee the room with the Grand Championship Cup, but his cape got caught on the doorknob and he ended up apprehending himself.

It was official. It was the end of the Fink dynasty. Fergus had brought shame upon his name. He had been cast free from his pedigree.

Fergus was escorted out of the Royal Canine Exhibition Center. For the first time in his life, he hid his face from the flashes of the cameras and the eager attention of the press.

He fled, never to return, leaving behind something *much* more precious than a trophy.

In a crate in a dark corner was the real champion: a whippet called Chariot. She watched as handlers and trainers departed with their dogs, leaving her alone and forgotten.

Until suddenly, the crate was lifted into the air. Chariot whimpered fearfully. But then she saw a face looking through the grille. It was her dearest friend, Simpkins. He couldn't bear to leave without her.

And they have been inseparable ever since.

Not since London has Chariot run through a tunnel or leaped through a hoop. She is blissfully retired. Her crate has been discarded, and she now lives with Simpkins in a quiet little home in the suburbs. She loves to nestle on his lap on the couch, and there's a small flap in the back door so she can go outside and lie in the sunshine whenever she likes. The two go on adventures together. To beaches. To rivers. To mountains and forests. And to Upson Downs.

And Chariot sits proudly beside Simpkins as he places his hand on Runt's heart.

Across the road, there is another public tribute.

A disused block of land has been transformed into a community garden bursting with exotic and fascinating plants.

It is called the Wally Shearer Memorial Reserve.

At the entrance, right beside the trail that leads inside, is a small plaque that reads: **_Everyone Deserves to Walk Their Own Path._**

In the center of the garden, there is a strange sculpture that puzzles all who encounter it.

It is not particularly beautiful. Or artistic. Or even useful.

It looks to be constructed out of scrap materials. It has a circular outer rim, with tin cans attached to it, which is connected to a metal box in the center. On windy days, the outer rim spins and creaks.

But sometimes, when the air is quiet and there's not a whisper of a breeze, people swear they can hear it turning. They can _sense_ it whirring madly on its own.

However, when they turn to look, it is always completely, mystifyingly still.

MEET ANNIE

Annie Shearer still lives in the town of Upson Downs.

As of today, she is twelve years old and still short for her age. She still has brown hair and brown eyes.

She still lives on a farm with her parents, her brother, and Grandma Dolly.

People in Upson Downs still think Annie is a bit different, but they love her for it. They have come to appreciate that everybody is unique, and it makes the world a more interesting place.

Annie Shearer has lots of friends, but she still enjoys her own company. Her favorite companion is still a dog, and his name will always be Runt.

The two of them are still famous the world over.

Their television commercial for Mush Canine Cuisine is shown in more than a hundred countries.

In it, they are inside a packed stadium, ready to compete.

Runt stands behind a white starting line. His coat is shiny, and he wears no blinders. Annie wears a purple polo shirt. She waves him through when the chimes sound, but Runt doesn't move. The crowd groans in dismay. Then, from the pocket of a tool belt, Annie produces a tin of Mush Canine Cuisine and cracks open the lid. Runt's ears prick up and he springs into action, completing the course in record time.

Waiting for him at the finishing line is a bowl filled with chunks of glazed, delicious meat. As Runt devours the feast, Annie cradles a large trophy and says: "Every dog will rush to Mush!"

It took four whole days to film it in a big studio. The camera operators had to hide under black sheets—otherwise Runt wouldn't move.

Max Shearer was on set for every moment, spellbound by the whole process. He pestered the crew with questions and filmed everything with his own camera.

After his viral success, Max's ambitions have moved beyond stunts. He now aspires to be an investigative reporter, visiting the most dangerous places in the world, producing hard-hitting documentaries. In his spare time, he also plans to make action films with lots of fire and explosions.

Runt is as popular as any movie star. He has been on billboards and posters and in print advertisements. His range of merchandise includes fridge magnets, tea towels, dog treats, chewable toys, hats, T-shirts, dog jackets, Frisbees, and even his own action figure.

And though his face is now on every label, Runt still isn't sick of Mush Canine Cuisine. It remains his very favorite thing to eat. To Runt, it still tastes like love. And kindness. And acceptance. And, faintly, of meat.

Interview requests and offers to attend competitions and conventions continue to pour in. Kingsley Krumpet the Third personally extends Annie and Runt a lifetime invitation to compete at the Krumpet's Dog Show.

Annie declines them all. She has no desire to be famous. She just wants to be at the home that she helped to save. It's where she and Runt are the happiest, and it's all she asked for on her birthday.

"Annie!"

She is being called outside by her father.

"*Annie!* Where's Annie?"

Annie and Runt step out into a bright, clear morning.

The Shearer farm is very different these days. For one thing, there are no longer any sheep. The herd of merinos chose to stay on Earl Robert-Barren's side of the road, and Bryan has never bothered to round them up.

Mostly because he is no longer a sheep farmer.

His paddocks are now lush and green and home to flowers and shrubs and seedlings and saplings and trees. Bryan Shearer's nursery teems with butterflies and dragonflies and bees and birds. He still invents and experiments in the same greenhouse, though there is no longer a lock on the door.

Anyone with a passing interest in plants knows about Bryan Shearer. His creative cultivations have won blue ribbons throughout the country.

And just like Wally Shearer's, Bryan's reputation among his peers inspires wonder and awe. They can only guess at his mysterious methods.

The funny thing is, Bryan's secret is exactly the same as Wally's.

He's learned it's the happiest plants that grow the healthiest leaves, the strongest stems, the brightest flowers, the sweetest fruit, the crispest vegetables, and the tastiest seeds and nuts. Bryan's plants, just like Wally's flock of sheep, truly enjoy his company. He talks to them, and encourages them, and occasionally sings to them, because plants adore music, even if Bryan still can't hold a tune. Some days he blows the dust off Wally's old gramophone and fills the air with sound.

They call him eccentric. They call him a maverick. They call him mad. They call him a genius. They call him all the things they used to call Wally Shearer, except Bryan has blazed his own trail, and he is just as happy as his plants.

"Annie!"

The whole family appears, wondering what Bryan is yelling about.

He steps out of his greenhouse carrying something behind his back.

"I know you didn't want any presents. But, well, it's a bit special, really, and I couldn't resist."

He brings his hands to the front, revealing an odd-looking plant. It has two large leaves at the bottom and one gnarly stem with six round bulbs growing out of it. He is beaming with pride. The rest of the family stares at it blankly.

"That is the ugliest plant I have ever seen," says Dolly.

"*Orchidaceae annieus*," says Bryan, handing it to Annie.

"What does that mean?" asks Max, who is, of course, filming.

"It means *Annie's orchid*. I cross-pollinated it the year you were born, Annie, and I've looked after it ever since. It's developed at its own pace, but just today I saw this—look."

He points at the end of a bulb. There is a slight crack at the end: the plant is about to bloom.

Annie peers at it.

"What does the flower look like?"

"I have no idea," says Bryan. "That's the exciting part."

Annie smiles, holding the strange knobbly twig with reverence.

"Thank you," she says. "It's really beautiful."

"It *is*?" says Dolly.

"Who is that?" asks Susie, whose attention has turned to an old car hurtling and swaying and bouncing down their driveway at considerable speed, kicking up a plume of coppery dust.

The Shearers gather by the farmhouse. They flinch as the car skids to a halt, crashing into a wheelbarrow filled with manure.

The dust cloud follows, shrouding the car in a brown mist.

"Sorry! Still getting the hang of driving the old girl again!"

Annie recognizes the voice immediately. She lights up.

"Bernadette!" she calls out.

As the dust settles, Bernadette Box climbs out of her rickety old car.

"I was hoping you would come!" says Annie. "Did you get my postcard?"

"I did indeed. I thought a visit was overdue. And, well, to tell you the truth, I enjoyed your company. Also, I wanted to introduce you to someone."

Bernadette holds the door open and waits patiently.

After a considerable pause, a small blue heeler puppy leaps and tumbles out of the car. She climbs to her feet and rattles her head, ears flapping. Then she sits obediently beside Bernadette's boots, head tilted to one side.

Susie melts.

"That is the most *adorable* puppy I have ever laid eyes on. No offense, Runt."

Runt takes no offense.

"I named her Annie," says Bernadette.

"Oh, my *goodness*," says Susie, melting further.

"Is it really her name?" asks Annie.

"Well, she's persistent. And kind. And determined. And quiet. And clever. And unexpected. So it's fair to say she reminded me of you."

Runt, usually wary of other dogs, wanders over to give the blue heeler a nasal inspection. Annie the puppy rolls onto her back and bats at the air with her little paws.

"I rescued her from the pound," says Bernadette. "She hasn't left my side since. We're good mates already. Looks like she's made another friend here too!"

The two dogs start to play. Annie the puppy yaps and chases while Runt spins and dodges and wags his tail.

"She's full of energy. Loves to chew on my—"

Bernadette freezes midsentence.

She has just noticed Dolly Shearer for the first time.

Time seems to stand still. There is electricity in the air again.

Bernadette is suddenly flustered and a bit coy. She glances down bashfully.

"Oh, hello," she says softly. "You must be Dolly."

Dolly doesn't answer, because something peculiar has happened to her too.

She stares back in a daze. Gobsmacked, almost swaying on her feet. Dolly the Dodger has finally been knocked out.

She blinks hard, down for the count.

"Me?" she blurts eventually. "Ah, yes. I believe so."

Bernadette blushes and stammers, nervous and shy.

"I'm Boxadette Bern. Er, Bernabox Bert."

"Bernadette Box," says Annie helpfully.

"That's the one," Bernadette says.

Dolly is blushing too. She softens, steps forward, and delicately holds out her arm.

"Bernadette, would you like to come in for a cup of tea?"

"I'd like that very much."

Bernadette hooks her arm through Dolly's so they're joined at the elbow.

"Do you take sugar?" asks Dolly.

"No, none for me, thank you."

"Of course not," says Dolly. "You look sweet enough already."

Bernadette laughs, and so does Dolly. The two start to walk toward the farmhouse.

Susie and Bryan look at each other and raise their eyebrows, smiling.

Annie watches Runt, who is zipping about joyfully with his new friend. She has never seen him play with another dog before, and it makes her heart feel full.

Susie, Bryan, and Max follow Dolly and Bernadette. As they round the corner, Bryan stops and turns.

"Are you lot staying here or coming inside?" he calls out. "Come on, Runt! Come on, mate!"

And something miraculous happens.

Runt's ears stand to attention. Then he trots past Annie

toward Bryan and the farmhouse. Bryan is astonished. Runt has *finally* listened to him.

Then, most unexpectedly, delirious with happiness as everyone waits for her to join them, Annie Shearer starts to laugh.

ABOUT THE AUTHOR

Craig Silvey is an author and screenwriter. His bestselling novel *Jasper Jones* was a Printz Honor winner, was shortlisted for the International Dublin Literary Award and the Miles Franklin Literary Award, and was named the Australian Book Industry Awards Book of the Year. His other books include *Rhubarb* and *Honeybee,* which won the Australian Indie Book Award. He lives in Western Australia with his family.

craigsilvey.com